D1590516

AGONY'S LODESTONE

LAURA KEATING

Cover & Illustrations by Trevor Henderson
Edited by Alex Woodroe

TENEBROUS

PRESS

Production of this novel was made possible in part by a grant from the Regional Arts & Culture Council. Visit https://racc.org/ for more information.

Published by Tenebrous Press.
Visit our website at www.tenebrouspress.com.

First Printing, March 2023.

Print ISBN: 979-8-9859923-6-6
eBook ISBN: 979-8-9859923-7-3

Cover art and interior illustrations by Trevor Henderson.

Jacket design by Matt Blairstone.

Edited by Alex Woodroe.

Formatting by Lori Michelle.

Printed in the United States of America.

ALSO FROM TENEBROUS PRESS:

For John,
for always being on my side.

And my sisters,
Kathleen, Breanna, and Anna.

PREFACE

WHILE *AGONY'S LODESTONE* is a work of fiction, the locations described within these pages are carved from the bedrock of reality. Fellow New Brunswickers will recognize certain sites and natural phenomena and I hope readers from those areas will enjoy the creative liberties I have taken. For readers from away, you might be surprised by how rich and uncanny this region truly is. Should you find yourself in the Bay of Fundy area . . . Tell 'em I sent you.

Laura Keating, Montreal, 2023

I

FACE IN THE DARK

BAILEY CALLED IN the early afternoon, which was unlike him. He never called. Aggie thought he might be in trouble again and she asked as much, but that wasn't why he'd contacted her.

"I found something." He sounded irritated with her moment of concern, but that could not overshadow his eagerness.

Aggie wished she hadn't answered the phone as she remembered his latest pursuit. "Wasn't that the point of the show?" she asked.

"Have you been talking to Alex?"

"He and Margot are camping with the kids. What did you find?"

"Let's grab a coffee." Bailey never answered direct questions. "Is Nellie's still open?"

"You're in town?"

"I'll explain over coffee."

She waited.

He waited.

"No." She hung up.

It was a hot day. The sea breeze through the open front door was no help as Aggie leaned back in her desk chair and waited for the phone to ring again. It was a Friday afternoon, but the light had a Sunday morning quality, dreamily pressing against the drawn living room curtains and playing at the dusty hem with long, golden fingers. The phone rang. She lifted the receiver to her ear without a greeting on the fourth callback. Bailey was quick.

"Aggie, please. It's her."

Aggie frowned. She'd been primed for more whining from a notorious victim, but for the first time in years, the man on the other end of the line sounded like her little brother. Her mischievous, sweet little brother who she had once known as well as herself but had nearly forgotten in the years since their family had been split from the top down like dry firewood under a heavy axe.

The floor fan by the couch ruffled the aisles of papers, finished edits, and printed transcripts stacked around the room. Her righteous annoyance withered to a husk as a feeling she had not expected swept through her like a cold wind: bitter loneliness. Her little brother.

"It's Joanne," he said. "I really found her."

He sounded scared.

The eldest Neilson sibling, Joanne, had been a swimmer of Olympic caliber.

She'd been breaking records and resetting them in unimaginable ways since the age of nine. Every race she'd finish a full seven seconds before her competitors, grinning and waving from her perch on the pool edge like a prom queen on a homecoming float. Medical researchers wanted to study her muscle structure, her oxygen intake. Rival coaches insisted she was cheating; there was no way this moon-face, country girl was winning without chemical enhancements. But she always tested clean because she was.

She was simply incredible.

There was a mural of her on the side of the Old Post Office in Lancaster Falls, the words HOMETOWN PROUD slashed across a faded scroll painted beneath her beaming face. You could usually find a crusty old "Justice for Joanne" flyer plastered below it, still clutching the wall twenty years on. Because a week after Aggie's twelfth birthday, two months before the 2000 Summer Olympics, Joanne took Doc, the family golden retriever, on a walk, and never came back.

Doc made it home fine.

The family had heard all the crackpot theories: It was the Russians, the Americans, jealous girls from her own team. They'd heard that she couldn't take the pressure and ran away, that there was a boy, a girl, aliens. They'd heard she was murdered by a transient, her parents, her siblings, by the mob . . . it got old. Browse any conspiracy theory website or unsolved mystery listicle, and she usually made an appearance.

Often, just like in her racing days, she took the top spot.

Their mother stayed in Lancaster Falls after Joanne disappeared, devout in her conviction that she would come back from her walk one day. Their father couldn't hack it and found a new job in Halifax that winter. It was supposed to be a trial separation, but a year after Joanne disappeared, he was introducing the three remaining kids to his new girlfriend. They had gotten a divorce without telling any of them. Another thing that just slipped away in the night.

Alex and Bailey were their father's best men at the wedding that September, along with their uncle Doug. Aggie sat in the audience. Julia had asked her to be one of her bridesmaids, but she hadn't wanted the attention. At the reception, they were surrounded. There were not many guests, but they all gravitated toward the kids, a ponderous explosion in reverse, questions and sympathetic platitudes spilling from their lips like warm champagne.

"You're all so brave."

"Have you heard anything?"

"I just want you to know how sorry we are."

Alex, Aggie's older brother—the eldest Neilson child now

that Joanne was gone—fielded questions no sixteen-year-old should ever have to handle while slowly guiding his little sister out of the throng. Bailey pushed himself deeper into it. He'd always been dramatic, but this was the first time Aggie had ever thought that might be a bad thing. He'd been Joanne's favourite, and now it felt like he was abusing that very special honor.

The voices all around grew louder as the DJ spat into his shoddy mic and turned up the music, the questions seeming to take on physical shape: big rough stones squeezing, surrounding, suffocating . . . Aggie was outside before she realised she was crying.

Alex shut the sliding glass door behind them, and the voices and music became muffled, like they were coming from underground.

"You can stay out here, Aggie."

They were on a tiny patio off the back of the hall, nothing out there except an ice-cream bucket filled with bloated cigarette butts bobbing in scummy brown water. Nowhere to go but down and only if you jumped. Alex checked that there was no one below and tipped the bucket over the edge with his toe. It hit the ground with an unlovely, squelching crash.

"It's too fast," she said.

"I know."

"Don't tell dad." Aggie was still sobbing.

Crickets chirped loudly out in the dark. Inside, she could see Bailey in the middle of a circle of men and women, all listening to the eleven-year-old like they had money riding on his every word. More than one person had brought him a slice of wedding cake. He looked extremely pleased. Aggie hated him.

"I'm not going to tell dad anything," said Alex with a sigh, jamming his hands into his suit pants pockets. He looked so much older and more tired than any teenager should. "He and Julia haven't even arrived yet." He glanced back over his shoulder to confirm this, and Aggie took a step back to the railing, away from the window.

"I don't want them looking at me."

"They can't see you," Alex assured her. "When you're inside the place with all the light, you can't see anything out in the black. Just like Nana's house."

The windows at their Grammy Agnes' house scared her. There were no curtains in her living room and at night Aggie was sure that there was something, someone, out there, waiting, watching, and that a terrible face would loom out of the dark, white teeth and lips grinning—

"Don't scare me!"

Alex laughed a little. "I'm not trying to. Now you're the face in the dark."

He gave her his suit coat when he saw her shivering and said he'd come back and check on her if she wasn't inside in half an hour. And he did. Her dad came out once. But every half-hour, for the rest of the night, Alex was there. Every time he came back, with a piece of cake or a new cup of Pepsi, she'd ask him if he'd seen what she'd been doing, the face she had pulled or who she had been staring at the longest. He'd shrug and say he couldn't see a thing.

"Fun to be the monster sometimes, right?" he said.

Alex was a really good brother.

A bell chimed sweetly over the door. The small, bright café smelled strongly of burnt coffee and fresh bread. The black-and-white checked floor beneath the round, wire-frame tables was spotless; the rotating cake display case softly reflected the natural light streaming through the large front windows.

Nellie's Bakery was only a short walk from Aggie's apartment, but Bailey was already waiting at a table in the back, puzzling over two mugs in front of him like they were chess pieces. There was only one other patron, an old man with a neat moustache reading a magazine by the window.

Aggie watched from the door as Bailey used a spoon to crossly poke the foam on one of the two mugs.

No one wanted to dislike their siblings, but it was like being away had amplified Bailey, and not in a good way. His hair was taller, jeans tighter, and his unseasonable leather jacket and scarf were so crisp it was like they'd never been moved in. His sunglasses—kept on—looked like they could have paid for a month of her rent, and his low, unscuffed boots seemed too good to touch something as base as the ground. It was like a costume; he looked conspicuous. But she guessed that was how brands worked. Noticeable was the point.

Bailey finally spotted her. He didn't get up, but grinned his lopsided grin. "Hey, you."

Aggie crossed the floor and dropped her backpack by the table. Bailey glanced down at the pack. His grin retracted by a molar.

"So, you're still doing that?"

She declined to answer. "When'd you get in?" she said, not sitting. She wanted to get a good look at him. He did not seem so nervous now. She could not tell which was the act.

"Flew into Halifax two days ago."

"How're dad and Julia?"

"You're the first family I've seen."

Pendle Bay, the town Aggie had moved to some ten years earlier, was only a five-hour drive from Halifax, a morning's trip if you got up early enough. She almost asked what he'd been doing for the past two days if not visiting their father, but she found she didn't actually care.

Bailey gestured around the café. "This is a cute place. Nicer than I remember. Got that authentic cottagecore vibe."

"Tell me about Joanne."

He hesitated. "Come on, just sit a sec. Can't remember the last time I saw you."

"I can."

"I ordered you a decaf latte. Extra foam and honey, right?"

8

That he remembered her order caught Aggie off guard. Bailey sighed. He sounded very tired. "You want to get right to business, then we'll get right to it. But don't just hover there like a storm cloud." He held a hand to the chair before her. "Please?"

Aggie exhaled slowly as she sat. The air conditioning was cranked to its fullest and goosebumps rose on her arms. She cupped her hands around the coffee and waited for him to begin. Bailey's knee bounced as he gave a quick look around the nearly deserted room.

"So, you know how my show was going to take me and my crew to different locations?"

"I don't want to hear about the show," said Aggie, sipping her coffee. "I want to hear about Joanne."

"Let me get to that."

The fucking show. Building a brand of brooding and tormented survivor of their sister's disappearance had been bad enough, but a few years back Bailey had managed to sell a pseudo-mystery hunter/reality show to one of those Used-To-Be-Educational-But-Now-Is-Aliens networks about his SEARCH FOR ANSWERS. He'd thrown a party for himself to surprise everyone with the news. He'd pinned one of his mock-up series posters on his kitchen door, so it was the first thing you saw when you walked into his apartment: their airbrushed kid brother, arms crossed over a tight green t-shirt as he managed to simultaneously pout and scowl at the camera, looking ready to serve up a righteous ass-kicking with the misty words "Someone. Knows. *Something*" shining out behind him like discarded *X-Files* promotional material.

Alex had laughed; Bailey got offended. Alex realized he was serious, and a fight broke out. Words were said, a punch might have been thrown, a glass of wine definitely was, and Bailey stormed out of his own apartment, leaving their mother to scold Alex and Aggie because couldn't they *try* to be more supportive, at least he was *doing* something, didn't they *love* their sister?

Their mother ended up selling off all the land she'd inherited—land that was supposed to go to all three siblings—to set Bailey up in LA while he worked out the details, as he called it. That had been two years ago. While Aggie still opened his infrequent emails, it had been the final blow for Alex. They hadn't spoken since. He even unfriended Bailey from all social media networks. Even Aggie had thought that was too far.

"They reworked it," Bailey went on, "so we'd also have a couple new mysteries each week. Staged but real too, you know? We've already filmed five episodes. Showing up to ask questions about Joanne but uncovering something else and we'd help fix it."

"You'd be the Winchesters."

"What?"

"Never mind."

"Like I was saying, they reworked it. Brought in a co-host, which pissed me off because it's my story."

"Our story."

"Right. Well, we were supposed to do filming around Lancaster Falls this Fall, but then there were problems with getting a crew up, some tax thing, they wanted to give Turner more camera time, I don't know. I called the producer about the changes . . . might've had some words."

"Are you going to be able to work it out?"

His heel stopped bouncing. "I got written off."

The words hit her like a cannonball. He went on talking like he hadn't just shot a hole through her chest, about how Turner, the new host, was a real prick but how they'd edit things to make *him* look bad, like he'd quit or had it coming, how it wasn't fair. Aggie recovered from the first shot and cut him off.

"You got fired."

"Written off, but that's why-"

"You got fired from a fucking reality show." She was having trouble keeping her voice down. "*Our* reality, that you

10

dragged all of us into, spent all of mom's money for. Before it even aired?"

"I'm going to get back in."

"How?"

"Don't act like you know how any of this works," he spat. "I have a hundred thousand followers on Instagram and twice that on twitter; you still have a landline."

"I may not know show business, but I don't need to be a proctologist to know an asshole when I see one, either."

The old man by the window barked a laugh. He cleared his throat when they looked around and snapped his magazine wider.

Bailey took a deep, calming breath. "I'm getting back in. I've already planned it out, building my own story arc from the outside." He sounded like he believed every word. "Everyone loves a redemption cycle, especially if they have something new to bring to the table. So, for the last two months—"

"You've been living in LA without work for two months?"

He had the good grace to be ashamed. Or maybe he'd just perfected the look; one could never tell with Bailey. "Dad's been helping out."

"Which is why you wouldn't stay with him."

"He generates a very negative environment."

Aggie glanced at the clock over the cash counter and sighed. "Guess who does work?"

"I've been building my story," Bailey went on with braced patience, like she was wasting *his* time. "Doing solo research, about my journey . . . and I found something. I actually found something."

Aggie pointedly sipped her coffee. He huffed.

"You don't care. Fine."

"Go to the police."

"I can't do that."

"Is it illegal?"

"No."

11

"Then why not?"

"It's hard to explain."

"Because the cops won't get you a second season?"

He didn't answer, and she knew she had hit on the truth. She got up.

"You should see mom before you leave. You owe her at least a visit."

Bailey looked hurt. "I'll be sure to tell her what a *huge* help you were."

Aggie scoffed so loudly that the waitress refilling the pastry display jumped. "Are you threatening to *tell mom on me*? Regress any further, Bay, and you'll be in Huggies."

He grabbed her hand. "Wait, Aggie."

"Let go."

"Just watch the tape."

"What tape? You know what, I don't care." The light from the sun illuminated his eye behind his sunglasses. It threw her. "What's wrong with your eye?"

He didn't answer but did at last let go of her hand. The clock over the cash register ticked steadily on. Bailey looked away. Up close, Aggie could see something was amiss. The shirt he wore beneath his jacket was rumpled, the collar looked stretched, slept in. His hair was styled but unwashed, it didn't quite stay in place the way she knew he would have preferred. Her fingers reflected briefly in the dark lenses of his glasses, but he gently brushed her hand away. He delicately removed the sunglasses himself. A yellow and purple bruise curled over his left eye; a purple mouse pushed up the soft skin beneath. It looked like it was healing, but it would have been a doozy of a shiner in its time.

"I fucked up," he said quietly. "But I wanted to come here, explain, make you see it wasn't all a waste of time. This is real."

Aggie's eyes roved down from his face to his chair. There was a slim leather satchel slipped over the back of the seat.

The hard black edge of a videotape peeked out the top.

II
LOST RECORDS

IT WAS SURREAL to see her flashy kid brother crouched in between her boxes of work and piles of papers, sorting out the knot of cables behind her ancient, dusty TV.

Aggie had entered her apartment first, quickly moving some coffee mugs and old dinner plates to the kitchen as Bailey had stepped inside with the wary tread of an archeologist entering a lost ruin. He'd said nothing as he navigated around the boxes in the kitchen and slipped into the living room. He'd waited patiently as she dug out her old VCR (the same one she'd had in high school) from under the neglected China hutch that had once belonged to Grammy Agnes but now belonged to the folded laundry forever piled on top. He didn't ask how she had managed to keep it for all these years: Aggie didn't lose things. She held onto everything.

Bailey lifted a single page from the top of the nearest stack of papers as she rooted around for the VCR cords.

"How's the editing going?"

"I keep busy."

"I guess."

Everything she'd ever worked on, she printed out. She'd done the proofs for hundreds of books, scripts, quarterly reports, and brochures. Copy edits on cookbooks, coffee table books, and fiction. Recently, she'd been hired out by several law firms to transcribe their dictated affidavits. Bailey set the page back, unconsciously wiping his hands on his jacket.

"Don't you have digital copies?"

"A power cut at just the wrong minute doesn't wipe out a binder. I like to keep things reliable, solid," she said as she pulled a tangled clump of cords from their nest behind the couch. "Just in case."

"Keep it real." He sounded both sincere and unconvinced. "I get it."

He had set to work setting the VCR up, running an old head-cleaning tape first to improve the tracking. He was taking no chances with the integrity of his find, and when he produced the tape from his bag, Aggie could see why. The casing was cracked, the label was a crusty yellow scab, the plastic window a dead, scummy eye. The filmstrip itself was, miraculously, in good condition. Smooth and shiny as a ribbon of black glass.

"Where did you get this?" she asked.

Bailey explained.

Two weeks ago, he'd gotten a DM from a guy who did groundwork at the nature preserve, Cannon Park, outside of Lancaster Falls. He was a new hire, taking over for the old coot who'd been the groundskeeper for the better part of forty years. The security cameras at the entrance of the preserve delivered their feeds to the groundskeeper station deep in the woods. They'd gone digital years back, with new cameras set up and feeding to a desktop computer. But the original wall of analog monitors had been so big it wasn't worth the expense to haul them away. So, there they sat in the groundskeeper hut, a glorified magnetic bulletin board for two decades.

About a week into the new job, the young guy started messing around with the ancient monitors and realised that there was still a tape in one of the machines.

"He plugs it in," Bailey said. "First time it's been activated in over twenty years. He grew up in Lancaster Falls and was as familiar with Joanne's face as anyone else in town; he recognized her right away."

"So why didn't he go to the police?"

Bailey looked over his shoulder, pausing his work. "He was scared."

He blew on the tape and fed it to the machine. It clunked as the static on the TV flickered to blue and then the picture trembled into focus with a brief, snarky buzz.

The black and white video was shot from overhead and at a slight angle, as if the camera had dropped on its mounts. Dark pine trees, a wooden map, and a rocky trailhead with a staked wooden sign reading "Hart Trail" were all starkly lit by an over-bright lamppost. A moth fluttered past the camera lens; a digital clock with date as well as time clicked away in the lower left-hand corner. Twenty seconds in, there she was. Just as Aggie remembered.

Joanne stepped off the trailhead holding something long and coiled in her right hand. She stopped at the edge of the woods to look around.

Aggie's hand found the back of her chair.

Joanne cupped the sides of her mouth, calling, although there was no sound on the tape. She ran one hand anxiously over her hair—and looked behind sharply, as though alerted to a noise. Hesitating, Joanne turned around and went back up the trail, disappearing into the trees.

Aggie got down onto her knees and shuffled closer to the TV, tilting her head as though she might see better, deeper through the woods after her sister. But twenty seconds later, she was back. It was the same thing. Joanne stopped, called, ran a hand through her hair, looked around, then went away. The third time this happened, Aggie noticed the collar dangling at the end of the thing in her hand.

"Doc slipped his collar," she whispered, like anything louder would spook the image of her sister into hiding, disappearing again. It was the night she went missing.

Aggie sat back, hugging her knees, and watched the loop

twice more. Her big sister left the woods and then returned to it, continually searching for the runaway dog. Aggie frowned. Why did the camera only record this minute? She knew that before digital, security tapes frequently got reused, especially in low-traffic areas—sometimes as soon as the tape was done, it would auto-rewind and loop back to the beginning of the film to start the record again. But a small fragment like this seemed manufactured. Did some . . . she didn't want to finish the rest of the thought, but her mind went there anyway.

Did some sick fuck do this? Edited the security tape and left it in plain sight? A clue for the moment he'd lured her away? Was she taken away or was she still in those trees? Her remains? A horrible hope rose in Aggie. Yes, it was likely they were. But could there be any evidence gathered after so many—

"Fingerprints." Aggie stood up suddenly. "Only you and the groundskeepers should have touched this tape. If there are more prints, maybe it could be whoever edited—"

"Aggie." Bailey tapped the screen. "Look."

The clock in the corner was not looping.

The clock was counting up in a perfectly regular beat, second after second, minute after minute. Aggie watched another cycle. The video showed a loop. She counted as she watched again. Twenty seconds of stillness; Joanne appeared; forty seconds later, she was gone. Time moved on and on. Little details that couldn't be replicated were back with each return of their sister: a strand of hair fell over her eye as she brushed her hand back across her forehead; the zipper of her windbreaker dropped an inch as she heaved a breath; the moth flying by the lens; the slip of her lip as she bit it slightly, anxiously, with her front teeth.

Bailey sat on the edge of an armchair beside the TV, careful not to disturb the papers that covered the seat.

"I've watched the whole tape, to make sure nothing changes," he said. "It repeats for six hours. At least, that's where the filmstrip ends. And this." He tapped the screen again: The date. Only two weeks earlier. The night the groundskeeper found it. "The camera had been recording all these years, just no one was watching."

"A programming bug."

"That's not how VHS tapes work."

They both jumped as a stack of boxes crashed in the kitchen. A man hissed, "Shit." Then, "Aggie? You home?"

Alex appeared around the corner and froze. He looked rumpled and exhausted—exactly like a man who'd been camping with a five- and seven-year-old. He saw Bailey. The corner of his mouth twitched. Aggie couldn't tell if he was holding back a sneer, a laugh, or both. He began to say something but whatever it was died on his lips as he saw what was on the TV between them. Alex stared for two full loops. When he spoke, it was like he was introducing them to an old friend.

"That's Joanne."

He started to cry.

Aggie made tea. Alex got a hold of himself as quickly as he'd lost it and went outside to tell Margot to take the kids home, he'd take the bus back tonight. The explanation Margot was owed was made plain when their kids spotted Uncle Bailey and vaulted out of the minivan, surrounding him and jumping around him like a couple of excited puppies. It took another twenty minutes to herd them back to their seats. Margot planted an understanding kiss on Alex's cheek. "Good luck," Aggie heard her remark from the door.

Alex came back inside. He glanced at Bailey and joined Aggie in the kitchen.

"Thought you were camping," said Aggie.

"Henry picked up a rash, so we called it early," said Alex. "Thought I'd drop by and say a quick hello, as we were passing through. See if you wanted to catch lunch."

LAURA KEATING

The kitchen table was mostly taken up by boxes of washed jam jars, clean plastic containers, and yet more papers, but Alex, who dropped by once a week and was used to the arrangements, cleared a small spot for himself and sat down unperturbed. Aggie began to explain Bailey's visit, filling him in on everything. When she'd finished, Alex crossed his arms and leaned back in the creaking kitchen chair. He had inherited their mother's height and their father's broad shoulders; the athletic build and dusty blonde hair were features he and Joanne had shared. Bailey and Aggie, along with the contrasting dark hair, had developed just the opposite; small and lithe, like they were made to slip through the thin places of the world rather than blaze a trail across it.

Alex sighed. "How much trouble are you in?"

At first, Aggie thought he was speaking to her. Then he looked around at Bailey, who was leaning, arms folded, with would-be nonchalance against the fridge.

Bailey saw him looking and shrugged. "I'm not."

"You honestly believe I'm buying the whole 'the groundskeeper was so scared he gave me this valuable tape' bit?" Alex chuckled. "In this economy?"

Bailey muttered something crude.

"And do you want to tell us what you were doing in Halifax for the last two days, where you've been hiding out? Where are your bags?"

"Airline lost them."

"Where are you staying?"

"Aren't you the least bit curious about the tape?"

"Right now, I'm interested in the immediate problem. You."

"Fucking cold, man."

"How much trouble are you in?"

Bailey actually stomped his foot. Like a child. "What's with the interrogation?"

Alex waited patiently, then repeated, more gently:

18

"Bailey, how much trouble?" When Bailey failed to argue this time, Alex went on. "You're broke. You haven't posted on most socials in almost two months. You don't have a YouTube channel for residual income, and your Instagram account is barely active—enough to show that you're still blowing through cash, keeping a 'look' alive, but no products. If you had any sponsors, they're gone now."

"You don't follow me."

"No, but CanoeDude1985 does. You think I wasn't keeping tabs on how mom's investment was going?" He let that hang as his jaw tightened. "Unemployed but still living large, trying to rebuild the bridges you'd burnt, you get this offer for the tape . . . Who have you been borrowing the money from? Not from any bank."

Bailey's face turned red, like he was biting on a hot coal. Then he looked away.

"How much are you in for?" said Alex. "That shiner says ten thousand?"

Bailey cleared his throat. "Forty grand. But the tape was only two g," he added as Aggie's jaw dropped and Alex threw his head back laughing. "It was an investment," Bailey went on, petulantly. "This tape can make it all right."

"How do you even spend that much money in two months?" Aggie said.

"Expensive tastes and expensive friends," said Alex.

Bailey's face went so red he could have stopped traffic.

"Not so friendly anymore, though, are they? Is that why you came back home? Somewhere to lay low while you make a digital copy to send to your old producers? Or were you hoping to get us in on it, sign over some life rights and sweeten the deal? Land a fat advance, pay off the brute squad, then bail on all of us again while you profit off our collective loss."

"What are you now, a cop?"

"No. Just someone with more than two *sense* to rub together." He grinned darkly. "Get it? *Cents*? Works on two levels."

"Save the dad jokes for the offspring."

"Did they follow you?" Aggie said.

"Who?"

"The nice men who want to break your knees."

"Oh, I thought you were talking about someone on Twitter."

Alex got up with his tea and headed to the window. Bailey crammed his hands into his jeans pockets.

"I don't think so. Maybe?"

"Maybe," said Alex.

"No. Only production knows where I'm from."

"Reassuring."

"Hey, fuck you."

It was possible a real fight might have broken out then, had the sound not interrupted them. Nobody moved. It came again: a hissing whine; electric, like an old radio searching for frequency. They followed the source back into the living room.

The tape was still playing, had been the whole time. After several loops of the same, during which time he never took his eyes off her, Alex sighed.

"We take this tape to the police, like you should have the second you got it."

"No goddamn way," said Bailey. "Not before I check out this location."

"Not a chance."

"That's the whole reason I'm here, don't you want to see it? Get a feel for what happened?"

"Of course, but it's not right."

"That's the whole reason why I'm doing this!"

The noise came back, louder than before. The tracking blurred worse than ever, a blizzard of static. Aggie hit the side of the VCR; Bailey hissed, "Careful!" The static and the whine worsened; Alex said, "Eject it before the machine eats it."

And it stopped.

The picture was clear again: the trailhead, the dark pine trees. A moth flew in front of the camera.

Aggie realised Bailey was right on one thing: The tape was important. He'd gotten himself into potentially very bad trouble, but that was his problem. If he had to give up his life on the West coast, so what? He could get a regular job here and hope whoever he'd pissed off never came looking for him. It was a full continent and a different country away. Right now, they had to do right by Joanne.

Aggie said, "All right, we go to the police," and made to eject the tape when Joanne came out of the woods again.

It was all wrong.

She was bleeding, and not just a little. Her blonde hair was plastered with blood, glistening like wet tar under the lamplight. Her face was streaked, her eyes wide and wild with terror. She tripped as she ran, skidding her already bloody hands across the gravel, screaming as she scrambled to get to her feet, and then out of the camera's eye.

"The fuck, Bailey?" said Aggie as Alex said, "Turn it off."

Aggie rounded. "You told me you watched the whole thing!"

Bailey's mouth opened and closed like a grounded fish. He twitch-stepped back from the TV, shaking his head. "I did. This didn't happen. This never happened."

"Well, it's fucking happening now."

The tape looped again. Not every twenty seconds anymore, but every ten, rapid fire. Alex demanded it off. Aggie hit rewind, going back one minute, three, ten, twenty. The tape clicked as it slammed into the beginning of the reel, and she hit play.

It was the same horrible scene. Joanne, terrified, injured, running for her life from someone, some*thing,* over and over, no sooner gone than drawn back to play out the chilling tableau again, and again, and again.

Alex hit stop. The screen went blue as the tape popped out of the player.

"Enough."

Aggie grabbed the tape before he could take it. She held it away. "It wasn't like that before."

Alex held out his hand. "Maybe you missed it."

"But this isn't what happened."

"We don't know what happened."

Aggie's arm jerked.

Bailey snatched the tape. He backed away from both of his advancing siblings, holding it over his head like a live grenade. "Aggie, you want to check the place out now?" he said. "You've changed your mind?"

She hesitated, then nodded. "Yes." Suddenly she found it was the only thing she wanted. She didn't know what was wrong with the tape, but there was nothing wrong with her eyes. Even twenty years too late, she had to see the place her sister vanished from the world, to see the camera that had made this tape.

Bailey popped it back in the machine and hit rewind. Aggie turned her head, not wanting to see Joanne screaming anymore . . . but Joanne walked out of the woods, leash in hand. A strand of hair fell over her eye as she brushed her hand across her forehead. She bit her lip. A moth fluttered by the lens. Over and over. The same as it had been.

Alex stared at the screen, all fight leaving him like water from a cracked cup. "What did you do?"

"I didn't do anything." Bailey heaved a heavy breath. "The cops haven't done shit on her case for twenty years. Do you think they'll suddenly bump her to the top of the priority pile for less than a minute of tape? Maybe a couple days with a cadaver dog but if they find nothing, they're done, the tape goes into a plastic baggie, and it's over. This province doesn't have the funds to care that much. But the three of us?" He raised his face from the screen. "No one cares more than us."

By its flickering light, he appeared so much older. His voice was quiet. "I'm not a monster, Alex. I miss her. I've always missed her."

"I'll drive." Aggie was already fishing around a junk

basket for her car keys. She found them, held them up looped around her index finger. Her expression brooked no argument.

Alex let out a long, slow breath and crossed his arms as he drew himself up and looked from the TV to the front door.

"We check the park out today," he agreed, reluctantly. "You'll both stay at my place tonight. Tomorrow, we hand in the tape."

Bailey, at last, nodded. Over his shoulder, their sister stepped from the woods and continued her search, calling out, unheard.

III

CANNON PARK

AGGIE ADDED FOUR granola bars, a lighter, and a bottle of water to her backpack. She never left home without her pack; she liked to feel ready. They left the tape on top of the VCR, Aggie locked the apartment, then they all piled into her Camry and headed towards Lancaster Falls, taking the winding highway up through the dense trees and across the rocky coast.

Alex rode shotgun. Aggie let the radio play. Bailey stared out the window. The drive to the nature reserve was a little over an hour, and not a word was spoken the entire way.

Cannon Park was roughly six-hundred acres of unspoiled land on the rocky coast of the Bay of Fundy. Fat harbour seals contentedly sunned themselves on the seaweed-covered red sandstone off the shore; herons strutted in the nearby salt marshes; deer moved through the trees like ghostly, ancient lords. The park's terrain rose at a steady incline north before ending abruptly in a sheer drop to the freezing Atlantic. The northern cliff face was not accessible to the public; the southern trails were more popular, at any rate, and offered the more beautiful coastal vistas.

Aggie parked, and the siblings got out of the car. It was a beautiful day; a clear blue sky with only a single lost lamb of a cloud drifting beyond the park, far above the bay. Sunlight glistened and leapt from the water. Families with sunburned children hiked the southern trails; young friends picnicked and fed the squirrels nearer the rocky beaches; older couples strolled, hand in hand, along the boardwalk in the cooling salt air. A perfect summer day.

After consulting the trail map at the entrance, they made a goal of the ranger's station situated along a winding service road. After speaking to the groundskeeper, they would make for the Hart Trail.

They started up the main path through the park's dark interior, past forest pools choked with ferns, towering spruce trees, and Ice Age boulders covered in mossy green shawls. Aggie's calves began to burn twenty minutes into the hike. She spent most of her time inside, virtually only going out to walk to the grocery store and back twice a week. Alex fared better; a daily morning jog and years of running after two very active little boys was not without its merits. Bailey, however, even in his slick boots, breezed up the steep hill with an unconscious grace. And to his credit, every time he had to stop for either Aggie to catch her breath or Alex to stretch out his back, he never said a word. After forty minutes, they turned off the main trail and onto a service road, ducking under a chain. The rusted sign in the middle of the chain squeaked, protesting, *Employee Access Only!*

There came a sudden boom. The ground shook. Bailey jumped, stumbling into and seizing a sapling as though its pliant branches might hold him. Aggie and Alex soldiered on, unfazed, up the hill.

"The caves," Alex puffed, passing Bailey. "Did you forget?"

Bailey relinquished his grip on the tree and slapped the sap off on his jeans.

"Yeah, I forgot," he said, falling back in step. "Sounded like someone dropped a spare mountain."

What he had forgotten was that the park did not earn its name idly. It was a tribute to the natural phenomenon that occurred as the tide broke against the north face. There, the cliffs were dotted with caves, some extending deep underground, nearly the length of the park. The result of the water rushing in, colliding in the caverns, was a boom not unlike cannon fire. The sound near the cave entrances was deafening; the tremors the waves caused, while not dangerous, could be felt throughout the park—especially when the moon was new or full, when the tide was highest, as it was today. As children, on clear nights, Aggie, Alex, Bailey, and Joanne had drifted to sleep to the voice of the ocean bellowing in the caves.

At last, a weathered two-room ranger's cabin came into view. Its moss-festooned roof and flaking wooden door were a welcome sight. The bugs were starting to bite. Aggie dragged her nails across the itchy lumps rising under the sweat of her shoulder. Her bra strap was also giving her hell. Round the other side, a John Deere tractor and an ATV with orange pine needles littering the cracked vinyl seat flanked a gleaming, silver rental car, engine still plinking as it cooled under the hood.

Aggie cocked her head slightly. Voices and a distinct, tittering laugh were barely contained by the cabin walls. There came a growl of frustration from behind her. Aggie began to turn, but Bailey stormed past, muttering obscenities. He jumped the two wooden steps in one stride and hit the screen door with the heel of his hand.

The older woman and a young man inside started as the door banged open. The young man, wearing a dun-coloured park services windbreaker, backed away from Bailey. The woman's look of surprise melted to a gooey smirk, her perfectly manicured hands relaxing around her iPad.

"Hello, Bailey." She spoke with a cultured, mid-Atlantic accent that Aggie thought had died out with Katharine Hepburn. "Thought you'd gone home?"

"This is my home, what the fuck are you doing here, Lynn?"

"Working."

"Hey, man, I didn't know you were off the show," said the young groundskeeper. A fresh patch of pimples was in full, greasy bloom in the middle of his forehead. He couldn't have been two years out of high school. "No refunds."

Aggie slowly climbed the steps. Deeper inside the cabin, a skinny dude with long blonde hair streaming from a faded black baseball cap wielded a small camera. The camera guy tipped a disinterested look over his shoulder at Aggie, then readjusted a pair of headphones on his head and continued filming the inside of the cabin. The groundskeeper shuffled his feet like a guilty child as Aggie noticed the image on Lynn's tablet.

"Is that the tape?" Alex stared down over Aggie's shoulder.

"It's just a couple pictures," muttered the groundskeeper. "Took them with my phone."

"This is exclusive property," said Lynn. She didn't seem to know they had the full tape. Aggie knew nothing of show business, but words like photography and location manager floated through her head. "Now, if you don't mind, we're on a tight schedule."

"We do mind, that's our sister," said Alex.

The woman's demeanour shifted yet again, like she'd just heard an amusing anecdote and was obliged to either laugh or appear aghast. Stick a cocktail in her hand, Aggie thought, and she'd look right at home. She gazed with faux-intrigued sympathy between them, putting pieces together. "Alex and Agnes."

"Just Aggie," said Aggie.

"Close the door," mumbled the groundskeeper. "Bugs are getting in." Bailey did so.

The cabin was bigger inside than it had looked from outside. At the back, where the groundskeeper cowered from Bailey, a row of dilapidated monitors sat on top of a row of old filing cabinets the colour of pea soup. Below the cabinets was a pile of fridge magnets; Aggie watched as yet another slid down the side like a small, plastic slug.

The old cabinets rattled together as there came another growl from deep beneath their feet. Lynn and the camera guy looked around with mild interest but were not as alarmed as Aggie would have thought.

"Didn't think you got earthquakes on this coast," said Lynn.

"Not an earthquake," said Alex.

"What is he doing?" said Aggie. The camera guy had silently crept to the corner and was steadying his small but heavy looking camera on his chest, aimed at her and Alex.

"B-roll," he intoned, eyes to the viewfinder. Lynn tipped a finger at them.

"I have waivers you can sign before we go to production."

"They won't be signing shit," said Bailey, "because this segment doesn't exist."

"This is the season finale, Bay."

"I want you to leave."

The cocktail smirk was back but that veneer of phony compassion was gone. "Oh, honey. I couldn't fill a Dixie cup with the fucks I give about what you want."

"Ma'am," said Alex, "you do your work. We won't be a part of it. We've just got a few questions for this young gentleman here, and then we're going to the police. About that." He pointed at the pictures slide-showing across Lynn's tablet.

To Aggie's surprise, Lynn shrugged. "Fine by me. Do you know how many of these cheap mystery series I've worked on that have had the authorities involved in one way or another? It's good for business. Gives the whole thing an air of legitimacy."

Aggie tensed. "Excuse me?"

The cameraman powered off his camera and slouched outside, the screen door squeal-snapping behind him. Lynn bunched her nose in a little bunny smile. "It would actually really help the buzz to have a case re-examined before we premiere. Get some YouTube true crime chasers to do free promo for us. Are you sure you won't consent to being on film? What's your twitter handle?"

Alex brushed past Lynn.

"You seriously work with these people?" Aggie said to Bailey as Alex began to speak quietly with the groundskeeper.

Bailey dug the tip of his tongue into his lower jaw and then clicked his teeth. He grinned. "Lynn, babe, we need to talk."

Lynn set her tablet on an old monitor and she and Bailey went to have a hushed but heated conversation in the other room. Aggie picked up the tablet and carried it to the window, watching the three-picture slideshow. The salt breeze through the open screen and the soft interplay of light and shadow wove against her face. The violent video they'd witnessed that morning was starting to feel like a shared hallucination, a bad dream conjured up in the heat of the moment. It was cooler here in the woods; the birds were singing. A sobering tonic. Aggie stared down at her sister; Joanne's upturned face stared resolutely back. Almost like she could see her.

The tablet was plucked out of her hands.

Lynn didn't even speak to Aggie, just got back to work and left the cabin. In the other room, Bailey had gotten out his phone; he looked pissed. It was only with the tablet gone, her hands empty, that Aggie began to process the images. She followed Lynn. "Hey."

The weathered boards of the front step sprang under her feet. The cab light of the rental car blinked and chimed as Lynn opened the door and pulled out a jacket. "Can I get another look at those pictures, please?" said Aggie.

"No," said Lynn, swatting a mosquito on her hand. Now that she'd learned she wasn't getting any rights signed over, she'd lost pretty much all interest.

"It's important."

"I'm sure it is." Lynn pulled out her phone and began texting furiously. The ground rocked again, bigger than any of the previous shakes. Aggie stumbled sideways, caught herself on the splintering handrail as the birds in the trees, mostly crows, cried and took to the air. Lynn caught herself with an elbow on her car, still texting. She glanced up at Aggie, watching her from the steps. She stopped texting.

"I'm not a monster, honey," said the older woman, with surprising gentleness. "I get this is your family, I do. But it's old news. We're just telling it again, trying to find something new. One of the thousands of times it's been told before."

With that, she beckoned to the camera guy. Aggie descended the steps and watched the two disappear down a narrow trail behind the cabin.

The cabin door squealed open. Alex trotted down the steps, a piece of paper clutched in his hand. "Got a map," he said. "The trail where Joanne disappeared is no longer open to the public, but the service road goes right past the old trailhead."

"The pictures Lynn has are different from the tape," said Aggie.

Lynn had three images on the tablet. In all of them, Joanne was looking directly up and at the camera. In the video, the same video the groundskeeper claimed to have taken pictures from, Joanne had never looked up once.

Alex was nonplussed.

"Just a couple frames we didn't notice," he said.

"We would have noticed," said Aggie. "It was like she was staring right at me."

"Joanne was here. That's what matters." Alex took a deep breath. "That's something that doesn't change."

Aggie understood his impatience and didn't argue further. Because she was impatient, too, here for the same thing. To see the place Joanne disappeared would make it real.

Once, there had been a real girl. She sat across the breakfast table, she hogged the couch, she took too long in the bathroom—a girl who told jokes so funny you laughed until your sides hurt, who never left you waiting after school because she was always on time, who sang during thunderstorms, who swam like the tide. For twenty years, that girl had been gone. Less than dead. Disappeared. Undone, mythologized. Graves could be visited, ashes scattered or held, but a disappearance ripped a hole in the world the size of a life, and through it sighed a terrible and uninvited wind, repeating a single note: *Gone.*

Gone, it whispered. *Gone,* it hummed. *Gone, gone, gone.* You wished them home, you wished them alive, and then you wished them dead, which hurt most of all. Either the melody began again, or you forgot they were real. Forgetting was easier. They became a somewhere rather than a someone, an X-marks-the-spot without a map. For years, Aggie had forgotten the real Joanne, the way she had laughed, fought, been. But now she might be real again, and it was all Aggie wanted. To trade the *Where* for *One*. She owed Joanne that much. To say she was sorry. That it had been her fault.

It had been all their faults.

"The Hart Trail signpost from the video had been removed,
but the lamppost was still there...as was the old camera."

IV
WHAT HAPPENED TO THE CAMERAMAN

THE SCALDING METAL playground slides winked in the September sun as Aggie slouched out the elementary school doors. Joanne stood by the ladder, her hands stuffed in her dusty pink polar fleece jacket. She didn't say a word as her little sister—head hanging, feet dragging—made her way over. Joanne picked up her bike and the two sisters started walking home. It was only lunchtime, but Aggie was being sent home early for fighting.

Though it hadn't been much of a fight.

Almost home, Joanne said, "What happened?" They had to walk on the road. Halfway to their house, the sidewalk disappeared along with the pretty houses, and it was either walk together on the cracked asphalt or single file on the skinny lip of dirt between the pavement and the soggy ditch.

"Nothing. We were just playing." Aggie was six, and not very good at lying.

"Is that how you play?" said Joanne. She had the day off, a special allowance from the school so she could train at the Aquatic Center in the city. She trained twice on Wednesdays, in the morning and the evening. She was on her midday break, supposedly doing the assigned schoolwork from her teachers to keep her marks up, but Aggie had it on good authority that the spines of those textbooks were in pristine condition. Joanne had been the only one home when the school had called.

"I was playing with the girls," said Aggie, scuffing her feet. "They told me to do it."

"You really hurt that kid."

Aggie gave it a moment's thought. "He deserved it."

Blake Ansley was a shaved-head little shit in her kindergarten class. He laughed at mean things, stole Fruit Roll-Ups out of other kids' lunch boxes, and pushed really hard. The teachers never caught him, they never did anything because he was the son of Mr. Ansley, the third-grade teacher. Teachers' kids could get away with anything. This morning, Aggie had nearly choked him to death.

It had started with a game of House. Aggie hated that game. Of all the things they could pretend, why would she want to pretend to be back at home? Kristeen Clegcorn said she had to play with them, or they weren't friends anymore. There were already three moms in this family, two sisters, a dog and a cat. What did Aggie want to be?

Aggie was the guard.

She sat outside the plastic house in the corner of Mrs. Kilburn's classroom, reading a book, when someone pushed her over. She knew who it was even before she smelled his weird lunchbox funk, like bananas and cheese.

Blake laughed, a big, red, sticky wad of someone else's fruit snacks rolling around his crimson mouth. The girls inside the house squealed in false terror but real delight and yelled to hurry inside, "It's a monster, it's a monster!"

Blake got into his role and began shaking the sides of the house, growling, "I'm going to kill you!"

So, Aggie did her job.

She pushed him as hard as she could to the ground. A look of genuine rage crossed his face when he hit the carpeted floor. He wasn't playing anymore. He fought back from where he sat on the ground, kicking Aggie hard once, twice in the legs. There was a lesson in those kicks: you don't stop my fun, you don't fight, you don't fight back. He wouldn't stop, so she did the straight-forward thing: She shoved him flat, sat on his chest, and wrapped her hands around his neck.

Blake tore at her hands, and she squeezed tighter. A look of bewilderment washed over his face, then he started to cry, bottom lip out and eyes pinched tight like a baby. She lifted his head and deftly hit it off the floor; thump, thump, thump . . . He cried harder, bawling, face going red and then purple as wiry hands grabbed Aggie's shoulders. Kristeen and Lacey stood by the door of the playhouse, staring. Blake sobbed on the floor and Aggie was yanked back and spun around, her teacher yelling that what she did was wrong, Aggie, so wrong, and to go to the office. But it hadn't felt wrong.

They had told her to protect, so she protected.

The faded plastic beads around the spokes of Joanne's bike plinked softly as they walked.

"Mom and dad will be really mad if they find out," said Joanne.

A cold wire twisted in Aggie's stomach. She hadn't been afraid of Blake, but she was very afraid of what her parents would do. She was considering running away, just for a night. If they were worried about her, they couldn't be mad at her. A pickup truck blew by, puffing back their hair and stinging their faces with road dirt. Aggie could feel Joanne looking at her.

"You're going to tell?" asked Aggie.

"Do you think that kid will mess with you again?"

Aggie shook her head. She was starting to feel ashamed. "I think he'll be mad, but he'll be too scared to do anything."

"Good," said Joanne. "Because if it happened again, I wouldn't want my ass on the line when mom and dad asked why I hadn't said anything the first time."

Aggie looked up, hopeful but unsure. Joanne stopped walking and looked down at her.

"You're my little sister, and you're not going to get a spanking because some little shit didn't know not to mess with you."

Aggie giggled. Casual swear words still caught her off guard, even though Joanne was twelve and that's what twelve-year-olds did—as far as she understood.

Joanne shrugged and kept walking. "It's forgotten, then."

They spent the rest of the afternoon on the couch, watching soap operas and eating ice-cream. Aggie's parents never found out about the fight.

"I owe you one," said Aggie after bath time that night, warm in her PJs as Joanne read Aggie a chapter from a sci-fi paperback she'd stolen from the drugstore. Joanne closed the book and smiled. Aggie thought she had never seen someone so cool in her life.

"You don't owe me anything."

Alex pocketed the map and made for the service road; Aggie stopped and looked around. "Where's Bailey?"

"He went after that lady."

The groundskeeper stood at the doorway eating a candy bar and staring down at his phone. His kingdom once more uninvaded, he had resumed his bored stewardship of the cabin. He rolled a sticky lump of chocolate to his cheek and, without looking up, lazily pointed a finger to the narrow foot trail Lynn had taken. "If you're going after them, tell them that area is off limits to guests."

The shadows between the trees were growing more grey and less green. The temperature had dropped, and the sweet smell of earth and pine was getting stronger. Clouds moved overhead. Aggie thought they would have time to either find the trailhead or Bailey before perhaps getting caught in some weather, but not both. Bailey was yet again demonstrating what was more important to him. So be it.

They chose the trailhead.

The ground further up the service road was deeply uneven, pocked with holes wide enough to snag a foot, maybe break an ankle in. Soon the way began to fade until there was only a memory of a road. The terrain was so rutted it was as though someone had dragged an enormous plow along it; years of winter run-off carving a network of leaf-choked streams and puckered scars in the crusty earth.

The groundskeeper had indicated less than a kilometer to a bend in the road and from there a shortcut to the trailhead, but it felt like it was taking a lot longer. Aggie tried to make the most of it, to enjoy the good sweat and the heat in her muscles. She couldn't remember the last time she'd been to the park, but she figured it was middle school. Every June, schools from all around the region would gather the kids for a walk around the nature preserve to blow off energy before exams and give the teachers a break after a long, cold winter trapped inside. They'd finish these walks with a picnic at one of the scenic overlooks. Aggie had not enjoyed much of her time in middle and high school, but she had enjoyed the day trips. She was a solitary type and solitary was the default state in nature. No one expected you to say anything or be around anyone. You could just exist; a group could walk in silence together and there was nothing strained about it.

Lonely, she thought, unprompted. Joanne had never been lonely. She had always been surrounded by friends and admirers. But all this time, after sightings at a roller rink in Miami, rumors of joining a cult in Winnipeg, she'd been so close. She'd been home.

She'd been here.

The thought crept up on her. Had she walked right by her sister's remains? Had she lifted her face to the warm spring sun, golden rays shining off the water, while her sister's bones lay cold and alone behind her in the moss?

"We're bringing her home."

Aggie lifted her head. She wasn't sure when he had stopped walking, but Alex was right in front of her, grim understanding hard on his face. She couldn't hide it from him: the guilt she was feeling and the fear of what might come after. The change it would bring.

"Should we be doing this?" Her voice barely made it out of her throat. "What if we disturb evidence?"

"We can't do any more harm than twenty years has already done," he said. "I don't expect we'll find a thing today, there's too much ground to cover. But if we do, we take some pictures and leave. Just the way we came."

"After all this time, I can't believe we're here."

"It'll be okay. I promise."

There came another gargantuan tremble from under their feet. It must have already been raining off the coast, churning more waves. She hoped they didn't get caught in it.

The bend appeared suddenly, like it had been waiting for them. They left the road and snapped through the ungroomed brush. The shortcut delivered them to the trailhead in fifteen minutes.

It looked haunted. Maybe that was just how Aggie felt it should have looked. It was badly overgrown, and the logs that had once lined the trail were spongy and splintered. The gravel trail seen in the video had long since washed away, leaving a muddy, unpleasant streak through the crowded trees—themselves naked and dying things with scabby trunks. The Hart Trail signpost had been removed but the lamppost was still there, as was the old camera. It sat atop the post like a fat little gargoyle, now mostly obscured by sticks and bird droppings, staring down at them with its scummed-over, cyclopean eye.

Alex let out a long, low sigh. He sounded as underwhelmed as Aggie felt, but he wasted no time. He started down the path.

It was even muddier deeper in: Trenches of mud and boggy puddles filled with dead leaves choked the way. They had to abandon the path for long stretches, squelching along the edges, ducking under alder and birch branches, stepping like giants around tiny spruce saplings. All the while, they kept their eyes open for larger hazards that would not have easily bent to the weight of twenty years: Glacial boulders which one might have climbed and tumbled from; fallen trees which might have crushed, pinned, and concealed one.

The muck was becoming non-negotiable. Aggie's sneakers were soaked, her jeans muddied nearly to the knees. The mosquitos were relentless.

Alex stopped to look around. "We should go back," he was saying, when they heard a voice shout, "I said, sit down!"

Alex and Aggie exchanged glances.

"That's Bailey," said Aggie.

The shout had come from due south, the direction of the cabin. Alex hesitated, not keen on plowing directly into the thick trees. There was another yell. He grunted. "Aw, hell," and they cut in.

The thick brush fought against them. Brittle twigs snagged their clothing, dead moss stuck in their hair and dropped down their backs in itchy bunches. The stand of dead pine trees cleared out suddenly, and they found themselves once more in the riotously green space of the hardwoods. Aggie tried to make sense of the scene.

Bailey stood with his back to them. The camera guy panted and whined; half laying, half slumped against a huge fallen log. Her brother looked pale and nauseous under his tan. It soon became apparent why.

Alex sucked quick air through his teeth, "Jesus."

Bailey's head snapped around. Confusion topped his nausea. "What are you two doing back so soon?"

"Back?" said Alex, but Aggie couldn't find her voice: The camera man's leg was backward.

Or at least the foot was. Below the knee was a pyramid of shattered bone, its brown marrow center poking out of the pink and white shards like a half-eaten tootsie roll. Blood soaked the man's shoe, slicked his hands—which haltingly clasped his leg and the ground beneath him.

"Got to change the bandage," the camera guy said,

weakly. He was fish belly white, his lips two trembling worms. There was no bandage. His shaking fingers, sticky with blood and pine needles, were trying to untie his sneaker—the one pointed directly at his ass. "Don't want it to get infected . . . got to change the bandage."

"Leave it," said Aggie, more forcefully than she meant. Her mouth tasted metallic. She rolled her pack off her back. "Don't touch it."

"Don't want it to get infected," he repeated, like a parent advising their child not to be late for a bus. She wondered if he had kids.

Aggie had taken first aid courses years ago, as part of her swimming lessons back when she had wanted to be a lifeguard. She had never formally learned how to treat a compound fracture—that had been at a more advanced level—but Joanne had taught her the essentials. They'd practiced with snapped popsicle sticks.

She'd never seen a real one.

Aggie's hands were steady, but her fingers shook as she pulled out the contents of her bag: a lighter, a spool of twine, Swiss Army knife, an external hard drive, a never opened plastic rain poncho, a notebook, a clutch of pens, a canvas shopping bag, her extra granola bars, a travel-sized sewing kit. She always left the house with something, she liked to feel ready.

She didn't feel ready now.

The shortest knife blade snapped neatly open. The canvas bag made soft zips as she cut it into strips and squares. She kept her eyes on her work, not the cameraman, her lips pressed tight with concentration.

"What do you mean, back already?" Alex repeated, eyes darting down to the cameraman then back to Bailey.

"What do *you* mean, what do I mean? You left!" Bailey was almost as ashen as the injured man. He did not handle blood well. He sat down, dizzy, and kept his eyes on his big brother. "Where's the groundskeeper?"

"What groundskeeper?"

"From the cabin!" shouted Bailey. "You and Aggie said you were going for help. Is Lynn with him? She went after you—leaving me to deal with this." He threw an accusing hand out. "And he keeps trying to get up! Oh, I think I'm gonna be sick."

"Head between the knees, Bay. And he's in shock. You too, by the sound of it. Hey, buddy." Alex knelt in front of the cameraman as Aggie layered a wad of canvas over the bone and then tied it in place with a longer strip. It wouldn't stay. Her fingers felt thick and clumsy. She tried again as Bailey took deep breaths and Alex took off his coat to drape around the cameraman, who was now shaking like a nervous terrier. "What's your name?"

"Duh-Duke."

"Nice to meet you. I'm Alex." Alex actually had been a lifeguard, earning his Nationals at sixteen and working all through university. He might have been squatting in his flip flops on the pool deck next to a kid with a skinned knee. "Took a fall?"

"Fucking root," Duke puffed, white lips sputtering. He pushed his hands against the base of the log behind him and tried to straighten his shaking arms, tried to get up.

"I need you to stay seated just where you are, okay? You're doing great."

"I'm going to lose my f-foot."

"No, no." Alex found a menstrual pad in the backpack and bottle of regular-strength ibuprofen. He tipped out three tablets, asked if Duke was on medication, and then handed them over. As Duke choked them down, one by one, Alex handed the pad to Aggie, dropping his voice. "Over the bone, then lay the canvas."

Her fingers slipped again. She was sweating. "I can't," she whispered.

"Yes, you can. Got those down, Duke?"

Aggie cut the pad in half with her knife, laid it on top of

41

the bone, and took a deep breath. In thirty seconds, it was a heavy, red sponge. She didn't remove it, laid the other half over top, and blanketed it with a large square of canvas. When that soaked through, too, she unrolled her spare clean pair of socks and began stacking those. By the second sock, less blood was coming through, so she layered yet another canvas square, this time tying the bandages in place, keeping the knots off the point of the bone. There was nothing that she or Alex could do about the direction of the foot, that would have to be sorted out at the hospital. But at least she'd slowed the bleeding and protected the injury. Alex poured a little water from Aggie's canister for Aggie to wash her hands, and then tipped a drink into Duke's mouth. The painkillers and shock had taken the edge off the pain, but he'd lost a lot of blood and was listless, his grey eyes as glassy as wet granite.

Bailey said, thickly. "Lynn should have made it to the cabin by now." He was holding his head. "She'll have called paramedics."

"You feel alright, Bay?" said Alex.

"Dandy. You done over there?"

"It's covered."

The cameraman grunted. "My traveller's insurance better cover this."

They waited. Aggie reorganized her pack; Alex sat with Duke; Bailey paced. Time dragged by.

At last, Alex got to his feet. "I'm going to see what's going on," he said. "Shouldn't be taking this long. She should have been back by now."

"Maybe she's just waiting at the cabin," said Aggie.

Duke was getting paler by the minute: eyes half-closed, face slick, lips dry and puffing out with every muttering breath, "Fuck this, man. Fuck, fuck, fuck."

"There was a real first-aid kit at the cabin," said Alex. "I'll come back."

"We'll all go," decided Aggie. "An ambulance will be on

its way to the cabin by now. If we're already waiting there, the paramedics won't have to haul a stretcher out to us. Duke, we're going to get you up."

There were no objections. Bailey stood rock-stepping back and forth between wanting to help and not wanting to be in the way. Aggie and Alex draped an arm each over Duke's shoulders and lurched him to his good foot. Alex got in front of him, ducked like he was going to hug him around the middle, and muttered, "Sorry about this." He rolled the injured man around his shoulders. Birds took to the air as a scream burst through the trees. Aggie spotted Alex as he lifted Duke in a fireman's carry and Duke fell to soft moaning. Alex started walking. Bailey spotted the fallen camera and carried that.

It was slow going. More than once, they needed to stop and clear a way through branches or navigate around obstacles Alex could not step over. Overhead, insects stirred; a deer watched their aching progress with indifference; mosquitos lifted out of the wet earth to whisper incessant greetings in their ears and pinch greedily at exposed flesh. After ten minutes, Alex was red-faced and breathing heavily. After twenty, Aggie suggested they take a rest. Alex leaned on a tree for a minute, took a mouthful of water, and they were on the move again.

Fifteen minutes later, Alex stumbled, one knee going down sharply, and Duke began to cry. Aggie helped the cameraman to the ground and after another brief rest Alex and Aggie lifted Duke between them, carrying him like they were moving a table.

Forty minutes passed. There was no sign of the cabin.

They had to stop.

"How do you get lost walking down a hill?" grumbled Bailey. He had stripped off his leather jacket and stuffed it into Aggie's backpack. He'd been in an extra pissy mood since a branch had snagged his t-shirt, ripping a hole the size of a thumb into the thin fabric.

"We're not lost," said Alex, gritting his teeth as he and Aggie set Duke down as gently as possible. The hard lines of his forehead stood out as he straightened up, back popping. He squinted into the trees. Sweat rolled down his temple. "And you're not helping."

They tried to make Duke comfortable, propping him against a wide tree. Alex once more wrapped him in his coat. He looked like death warmed over. He had stopped making any sound; his skin was grey and cold, his pulse very rapid. Aggie wasn't sure if a person could die from shock, and she didn't want to find out.

But bleeding out was a possibility. The bandage was soaked through.

Bailey made a face. "Looking brutal, man."

Duke said nothing, only shivered and stared.

"We've been heading south this whole time," said Aggie reasonably, talking past Bailey's bad attempt at levity. Bailey walked by her, running his hands through his hair as he paced the area. "If we've passed the cabin somehow, we'll still end up at the park entrance." But an uneasy, dreadful knowing was creeping into her heart: they should have been there by now. She tried a smile. "I bet we're just a few meters out."

"I hate to break it to you." Bailey stopped his pacing and made a small turn on his heel, staring around the small clearing. He crouched and picked up a discarded strip of canvas. "I don't think we've just been going south."

No, Aggie thought, turning on the spot, taking in the trampled ground, the lifted tree root, a piece of wrapper from the adhesive side of the pad.

They were back where they had started.

"Impossible," said Alex.

"Well, we didn't walk backwards," said Bailey as Alex said something rude.

Aggie inhaled and raised her chin, gazing into the treetops, between the branches to the sane blue sky. She let out the breath.

"Stop fighting," she said, interrupting her arguing brothers. "In terms of fuck-ups, this could be worse. We're still near enough to the cabin, right? I'll go alone this time."

"I should go," said Alex.

"If the cabin is so near, then where are the paramedics?" muttered Bailey, petulantly.

"It's not a contest, Alex," said Aggie. "I said I'd go."

"I'll be there and back fast," said Alex.

"You can't do everything."

"They should be calling, looking," said Bailey.

"You're better at first aid," said Aggie. "Stay here with Duke, do what you need to do."

Bailey threw a canvas strip. "Why aren't they here?"

Alex rounded on Bailey. "Stop whining!" Bailey flinched back. Alex's voice was low and harsh, his eyes hard. "We're all here because of you. You said it's about Joanne, but at the first chance you went chasing your career again. Because it's always really about you. We've got a real problem here, and though it might be beyond you to be responsible you can at least be helpful and shut the fuck up."

A hard silence fell between them. Bailey opened his mouth—to fight or defend himself, Aggie never knew. Bailey's eyes roved over Alex's shoulder and his brow dipped in confusion.

"Where's Duke?"

Aggie and Alex looked around.

Duke was gone.

They did not immediately call out or exclaim; their surprise was too great. Unknown seconds passed. Bailey walked around the tree Duke had sat against, looked up the side of it—as if the man they'd been carrying for over an hour would be perched in the branches, hair hanging around his face as he grinned down at them. But there wasn't even an indentation in the moss where he'd been sitting.

He was just gone.

"Duke?" said Alex, but without real gusto.

A light began to flicker around the tree roots.

Bailey stepped back from the tree. The place where, moments earlier, there had been a man, started to glow.

The three unconsciously drew closer together as the glow grew brighter. It thrummed like the cracked door of a furnace. The strip became hot, blinding white light, like a magnesium ribbon on fire. From the blinding flare, a sound began reverberating, beating out of the light. The sound grew to a scream, it rose and wavered and suddenly the man was back, panicked and shrieking. He was not solid but made of white-hot noise, blazing white. His eyes rolled, crazed with terror. He clawed and reached for them, fingers rictus stiff, crying and panting and making no progress. He lifted his face, screaming still, skin peeling open and sloughing off like melting wax, like burning celluloid.

They ran.

Aggie tore through the forest, hurdling over fallen trees, rocks, and roots as she blindly tried to put distance between herself and the screaming white mass. The sun flickered overhead like a strobing flashlight through the canopy. She ran harder, but the screams only grew louder, closer. Alex crashed past her, shoving her shoulders as he did to get her to move, run, run faster. Bailey was right behind them, shouting nonsensically. Suddenly, Alex stopped, skidding on pine and leaves, arms pinwheeling as he did an about-face. Bailey just dodged him, but Aggie slammed into him. They both crashed to the ground, knocking the wind out of Alex. He gasped flatly. Bailey grabbed Aggie, then Alex's arm, tried to pull him up, to keep running, but Alex hauled Bailey back down sharply.

"*Wait.*" His voice was like dry leaves. "Listen."

Blood hammered behind Aggie's ears; her heart banged in her chest like a pneumatic piston as she got up onto her elbows and looked all around. Bailey heard it now, too. The screaming was coming from all over. But it wasn't Duke's terrorized shrieks. The woman's voice sounded raw, agonized.

"Lynn?" shouted Bailey—or tried to shout. The plea for help came again, this time from far behind them. Aggie shook, too cold and too warm at the same time. Alex was frozen, his eyes wide and watchful as the voice rang out from everywhere.

"*Pleeasssee!*"

Bailey grabbed his head, hands on his ears and hiccupped, big wet tears rolling from wide eyes down his face. "What the *fuck*."

The screams were already growing fainter. Then, all at once, they were gone.

Alex sat up, watchful and listening over Bailey's confused crying. Aggie wanted to tell him to get a grip, to say it wasn't about him, but she couldn't muster up the energy. Old habits overrode all sense and she put an arm around her little brother. He turned and sheltered his face in the crook of her neck, tears soaking the collar of her t-shirt. She rocked gently, side-to-side, as much for herself as for him. They could no longer hear the screaming, but she'd never get away from the sound. It would echo in the deep chambers and locked places of her heart forever, coexisting with other foul winds from other more terrible storms.

"The sound grew to a scream, and suddenly the man was back, panicked and shrieking...made of white-hot noise, blazing white."

V

BAILEY MAKES A BREAK

A GGIE WOKE TO her door opening. She had slept through the beginning of the fight, but now the raised voices rushed around her darkened room like a pair of duelling hawks. She didn't need to hear the beginning to know what was happening: Joanne was home late again. Bailey stood at her door, a skinny silhouette in Ninja Turtle pajamas. They locked eyes and without a word he scampered over to her bed, her duvet already lifted like a great wing under which he might nestle.

"Mom's going to kill Joanne," he whispered, tucking his knees up as Aggie dropped the cover.

"No, she's not," said Aggie with the profound knowing of a ten-year-old. He was whimpering. She hugged him and he closed his eyes tight; her eyes remained open.

"She'll kick her out."

This was a possibility. Aggie said nothing as the muffled-loud voices turned to screeches of "Get out of my room!" and bellows of "No! No! No! This is *my house!*"

Aggie slipped her hands over Bailey's ears; she tried to press her shoulder into the ear that wasn't deep in her pillow ... but gave up soon thereafter and resigned herself to listen.

Joanne had been out late with her friends again. She did not have a swim meet coming up, but this was one of the two excuses their mother used to rage every time she came back even a half-hour after curfew: School, swimming.

Their father's voice now, a low, exasperated rumble. He didn't last long. His stomps back down the hall shook the floor, and the slam of their parents' bedroom door rattled the window.

"Get out!"

Aggie hummed deep in her chest, hoping to dampen the yelling as she held Bailey tighter. It felt good to have someone to take care of, someone who she needed to be strong for. She couldn't understand her mother's rage—although she'd heard all the accusing rationale: Ungrateful; athletes had to be better; bad friends; disrespect; slut. But what she couldn't understand even more was how Joanne kept doing this. At ten, it seemed so simple: Couldn't Joanne just be good? Just don't make mom mad, don't poke the bear, don't go out, don't make me have to listen to this. Hot tears sprang to her eyes as she pushed the hurting thoughts down, down into a burning pit in her heart. The hard fragments melted there, and if she allowed herself to she knew she would be able to reshape them, to remake them. She wouldn't let the hard bits cut her apart, but she would let them surface, she'd wear them. Her perfect armor.

Something shattered in Joanne's room. Their parents' door banged open. Heavy footfalls down the hallway, their father's voice thundered as Joanne cried, *"T-That wasn't yours!"* and their mother's voice rose, moving down the hall, dragged by their father. *"UNGRATEFUL BITCH!"*

Their parents' door snapped shut. Heated but muffled voices droned behind the thick walls. Across the hall, Joanne was crying. The door to her sister's room closed, but the sobbing did not stop.

"It's over," Aggie whispered but Bailey did not reply. He was pretending to be asleep for her. She appreciated it. She kissed his forehead, and eventually they both really did drift off.

The next morning, the family had breakfast together. Their mother made toast and talked above the silence of

Bailey and Joanne like it was just another typical morning. In many ways, it was. Aggie tried to play along, talking animatedly back, trying to keep her happy. Alex came home from his paper route in time to grab an uncooked Pop-Tart and his bookbag before heading back out the door with the rest of them for the walk to school.

On the road, silence fell. A block from the elementary school, where Aggie and Bailey would break off with the older two heading on to the big school, Joanne cleared her throat. She had not said a single word all morning.

"Where were you?" She was looking at Alex.

"In my room," he said.

"And you couldn't hear that shit going on?"

"The whole country could hear that."

"And you just lay there and let it happen?"

"What do you want me to do?" he snapped. He sounded like their father. "It wouldn't have helped, and I had to get up at four-thirty this morning."

"A paper route, really great excuse," she said. "You're my brother, you're supposed to be on my side."

"I'm not going to fight your fights for you."

"I shouldn't have to fight them either. You don't get this shit when you go out!"

"Please."

Joanne looked down sharply at the small voice at her side. Bailey kept his eyes to the sidewalk as he plodded forward, scuffing his rubber boots on the pavement. "Please stop fighting."

Joanne knelt and lightly pulled his arm, so he'd stop walking. She squared his shoulders to her. "Hey, hey? It's okay, Bay. Look at me, it's okay." She tilted his small, pointed chin up so she could see his face. A tear rolled down his cheek. "We're not fighting, we're just trying to find solid ground between us. It's what brothers and sisters do."

"I'm sorry," he said.

"Nothing to be sorry for."

"I'm on your side."

"Aw, I know you are," she said, and she drew him into a warm hug, swaying tenderly as they each closed their eyes. "Thank you."

Alex stood back, impatiently looking up the road to their school. Aggie wanted a hug, too, but said nothing. This wasn't about her. She was the little sister but also a big sister and if they believed she was okay she would be. They all would be. She knew she could look after herself.

"We've got to get going," said Alex.

"Go where?" said Aggie. "We've been taking a five-minute walk for hours."

Alex ran both hands through his hair. Bailey had moved away from Aggie and was sitting cross-legged on the forest floor, head down, not making a sound. She was starting to feel like a character in the old Tom and Jerry cartoon, on an endless, repeating chase through a living room: chair, table, mouse hole; chair, table, mouse hole. The issue there was usually resolved with a huge wooden mallet.

She touched the smile forming on her lips and wondered how close she was to snapping.

There was a tiny whine and the rattle of canned voices. A glow lit Bailey's face from beneath. Aggie felt her heart leap . . . but he had just turned on the camera. Like moths to the flame, or perhaps in that prehistoric instinct to seek fire and light in times of hardship, Aggie and Alex gathered round to watch the viewfinder.

What they saw left them all cold.

The video began as Lynne and Duke left the cabin. Lynn trudged ahead taking notes and occasionally turning to respond with a great deal of irritation to a comment or question from Bailey who chased along after them. After a minute, Aggie and Alex joined them.

Alex spoke to Lynn, pointing in the direction of the road. Time and place jumped around as the camera rolled and then was turned off, rolled and turned off. During the last roll, the camera gave a sudden lurch, shooting skyward, and then tumbling into the moss. There was a brief shot of Duke's twisted, broken leg and then Lynn's face filled the screen, looking sick. The camera jostled as she peeled the strap up, over, and off Duke's shoulder. She set the still-recording camera aside, on a slight angle, facing the clearing . . . and madness broke out.

Two versions of Lynn jogged off in different directions; a third stayed a minute longer, talking to Duke, before also leaving abruptly. Alex and Aggie took off after this Lynn as Bailey stood back from Duke, telling the cameraman to just take it easy, to sit still. As Bailey tried to calm Duke down, Alex and Aggie appeared from the other direction. Bailey whirled around, confused and the camera was lifted up. Duke's face filled the screen, teeth gritted, and the camera was powered off.

Blue light soaked their faces. There was no more. Bailey switched the camera off.

When Bailey spoke, his voice was very soft.

"Let's try again."

They walked in silence. It was not a reflective or even fatigued quiet. It was the quiet of faraway thoughts and hollow fear. Aggie couldn't quite feel her legs and kept her eyes turned down to see where she was stepping. After a while, doing so made her think of tripping, and of Duke tripping, breaking his leg, and then—She stopped.

"You okay?"

She caught Alex's eye. He stood staring back at her. She glanced over his shoulder to Bailey, the powered-down camera still in his hands. She didn't want to make anyone worry about her. Now was not the time to think or to talk, it was time to move. They would make sense of things later. She nodded and took a step, stowed this idea away, a hopeful and bitter tonic: Later.

They used the sun—now low in the sky—to orient themselves and when still they did not emerge at the cabin or park entrance, they sat down again.

Alex could not sit for long. He got up and began walking in circles, cupping his hands to his mouth and shouting. He tried to keep the panic out of his voice, but Aggie could hear it edging in, softening the borders like rot in good timber.

No one called back.

The sun was setting. There was a deadfall nearby. Aggie started dragging branch after branch to a thick maple tree and there leaned them against its broad trunk, roughly creating the shape of a short tent. Then she got to work laying more branches down inside.

"The ground is softer," commented Bailey from where he sat cross-legged nearby, watching her construct this mattress of sticks.

"But wet underneath," she replied, tucking a strand of hair behind one ear. "It's summer, but at night on the Atlantic coast, the dew from the fog will be bad."

"I'm not a tourist, Aggie," Bailey reminded her. He sounded almost sad. "I'm from here." He paused. "Where'd you learn how to do this?"

She pushed on the springy branches, continued to arrange the lean-to into shape. "Did the proofs on a survivalist manual couple years back," she said, not looking up. She retrieved her Swiss Army knife, bent open the saw blade, and handed it to him. "Gather as many spruce branches as you can. Only cut from dead trees. There's too much gum in live ones, you'll be cutting for hours."

Bailey didn't argue but got to work, sawing at and gathering arm loads of spruce from the deadfall while Aggie built up the walls, leaning heavy branches and weaving flexible alders and coniferous between. It was good to have something to do with her hands, a craft to focus her mind and give her a purpose.

The sun was quivering on the horizon when she finished

stuffing her woven structure with leaves. In the small, damp clearing she'd made from plucking those leaves, she assembled a modest tinder pile of twigs, birch bark, and old man's beard and then crafted a log cabin around it. She started with dry sticks the size of her thumb, laying them two-by-two, and worked up to wrist-sized logs which she'd broken off the deadfall with a good stomp of her heel. Twisting a length of birch bark into a drooping sceptre, Aggie set the tip ablaze with the lighter from her pack and anointed the tinder with flame. As the fire gained some confidence, she expanded the damp ring of leaves surrounding the firepit, raking her fingers deep into the mushy, brown earth in a two-foot radius. Millipedes, spiders, and beetles hurried from their dark homes only to disappear underground again. There was no digging down to the dirt here; the soil was a memory under undisturbed years of fallen leaves.

Aggie tucked her freezing, filthy hands under her armpits and stood up, satisfied with the camp she'd made. Bailey returned her knife and then squatted by the fire to warm his own soiled hands. Aggie spied Alex sitting on a log, staring back the way they'd come. She did not know how long he'd been there. She roamed from the fire, stepped over the log, and sat down beside him.

"My phone." His voice was rough. Without looking at her, he passed her his cell. She turned it on. The screen was all panicked static; flashes of his wallpaper—Margot's white teeth, Jack and Henry's tussled hair—occasionally broke through, but otherwise it was visual noise. She gave it back.

Alex pocketed the thing. He turned his face up to the darkening sky. At length, he said, "Margot's going to be so worried. The kids."

Aggie put her arm around him.

"I don't want to scare you," he said. "But we haven't moved at all." He pointed off to their right. "The tree we leaned Duke against is only about fifteen feet back that way."

It was getting too dark to see through the trees, but he

didn't have to show her. She believed him. He went on and she let him. Talking was helping him not think too much.

"Time's moving on," he commented, gazing up at the star wheel unfolding over them. "The world is carrying on, we're just . . . in a pocket." Alex let his eyes come down to the dark trees, but what he saw seemed further away. "Do you think this is what happened to Joanne?"

She knew her brother, and she knew that he wasn't really thinking about their sister right now but of his kids growing up, getting old, wondering what had happened to their dad. Would they come looking, too, for his bones here? Would this place have them all?

"No," said Aggie, firmly, and although she couldn't be positive, it felt correct. "The tape we saw was a forty-second loop with real-time still ticking along. We haven't been repeating ourselves out here."

"We think."

"Ag?"

She pulled away from this troubling thought and turned around. Bailey was putting more sticks on the fire. "Come on over and get warm, you guys. Maybe we can roast one of Aggie's granola bars. I'm starving."

They each had a granola bar—unroasted—and a mouthful of water. It wasn't nearly enough, but the rest they saved. They did not bother adding more wood as the fire was reduced to a pitiful pile of embers, and the three crawled under Aggie's lean-to. Alex, who had lost his jacket when Duke vanished, took the deepest, warmest spot by the tree. Bailey took the middle, and Aggie the edge. She got Bailey's leather jacket, and they spread Aggie's rain poncho out over all; it did nothing for warmth but at least it kept the damp off. It was a tight fit, but in the end they managed to sardine themselves together and were passably warm, if uncomfortable.

"No way I'm sleeping tonight," muttered Bailey. But in the end, sleep found them all at one small hour or another.

Aggie dreamt in shallow fits, never fully unaware of the hard mattress, like broken finger bones, beneath her. In her dream, she was falling and after she had fallen, she could not get up again, as hard as she tried; pushing up against the pressure on top of her until her wrists snapped and the skin was rubbed bloody from her back. A scream welled up in her throat, but her mouth was packed with mud, leaves, water, filth. She could not breathe, couldn't move. She would die unless she opened her eyes.

The dark was so complete she wasn't sure that she was awake.

Her brothers' breathing, slow and deep, pulled her the rest of the way to reality. They seemed to be asleep, and she didn't want to wake them from the rest she knew was hard-earned. She remained still and moved her face just enough to see through the sticks at the top of the lean-to. The sky was a little brighter than the forest floor. It would be dawn soon.

A twig snapped.

Aggie moved her eyes.

There was a woman standing by the firepit.

Aggie could not see her face, could not see most of her in the dark. The fire was nothing more than a few hot embers and ash; it provided almost no light. Her back was toward the lean-to, her head down, her shoulders moving up and down in quick shivers. Aggie began to sit up, nearly called out, thinking it was Lynn, that she was cold or crying. Then she heard the low, wheezing laughter.

It clucked from deep in the woman's chest, like two stones knocked together. Her hair was matted and lank, her clothes ripped and wet, her fingertips raw and bloody like she had tried to claw her way out of something. She must have wandered by their shelter on her way into the camp but had not seen them. All at once, Aggie knew that she *could not* see them. She couldn't understand how she knew this, but it was not a matter of distance or dark: This apparition did not occupy the same space as them, and wherever she had gone or wherever she was from, Aggie did not want to know. She did not want to be seen by her, lest she be dragged back with her.

Aggie held her breath, her whole body shaking—no, she realised, it was just another tremble from the Cannon Caves, one so small she wouldn't have even felt it were she not lying down, so still, so petrified. The figure moved, a dead-armed rolling gait, dragging one foot in front of the other until she was lost from sight, vanished into the darkness between the trees.

As the sun rose, weak and pink, and the dawn chorus went mad, Aggie, Bailey and Alex crawled from their shelter, staggering with cold and stiff limbs. Aggie rubbed some warmth into her fingers and restarted the fire. They split the last granola bar and tried to not think about what the day would bring. Aggie scanned the trees and began to doubt that there had ever been a woman at all.

VI

ALEX TAKES A DIVE

"YOU EVER HEAR about the stone tape theory?"
It was almost noon. They hadn't stopped walking since they'd broken camp. Alex had taken the lead, followed by Aggie. Bailey had been slowing as the day wore on; his feet were hurting. While never truly stopping, they'd occasionally take the quick breaks for him to pad the side of his boots with dry leaves. They took the opportunity of those brief reprieves to look around, see how far they'd gone. Sometimes it was depressingly little; sometimes, it was nowhere at all.

"I heard about it when we were going to do a one-off episode down on this haunted farm in New Hampshire," Bailey said as he took another step, wincing at the fresh blisters. "The idea is that certain types of rock can 'record' energy, thoughts, and emotions. Given the right conditions, it might replay. A ghost is just that recording, played again and again."

"Fun," intoned Alex. He smacked a mosquito on his arm; it popped like a tiny, bloody balloon.

They had given up on the cabin and were trying for the trailhead today, back the way Aggie and Alex had come. They were, at least, making a little progress. After passing their own campsite three times, they abruptly found themselves forty feet north of it. Alex had spotted the lean-to through the trees behind them as they stopped for a water break. They'd been so happy they'd danced.

"This whole area is geographically unique, you know?" Bailey went on. "Only geopark of its kind in North America. Here, in this little city, is the exact spot where three continents collided and then broke apart, the whole ocean spilling between them. You can paddle up the St. John River and see the spot where North America, South America, and Africa split. There are Precambrian fossils here—that's a *billion years old*. Before the Cambrian explosion, before life as we know it. The sort of shit you can only measure in Deep Time. Right beneath us."

"Super," said Alex.

"When did you become an amateur geologist?" said Aggie. Her stomach felt like an empty rubber bag rubbing against itself; her tongue like a dead slug.

"I research my material." Bailey sniffed. "I take pride in my work."

Alex called for a full rest half an hour later. They each had another mouthful of water—not enough but also too much if they were to keep going like this.

"Highest tides in the world."

Aggie looked around at Alex. He snapped a twig in his hands, found another, and broke it the same way. He seemed to be talking to himself. "That's what we've got all around us. Highest, fastest tides in the world."

You didn't grow up in the Fundy Bay area and not know this fact. All the same, Aggie nodded along just as she had nodded along to Bailey's little geography lesson.

"Magnetic Hill," Aggie added. She was referring to the road near Moncton, created and discovered wholly accidentally when locals were laying a cart path back in the nineteenth century. Local lore said a barrel fell off a cart and appeared to bounce back up the hill, and it became a community amusement. Even photographs of the road were hard to get your head around, impossible to accurately determine the highest point just by looking. Once on a family road trip to the nearby Magic Mountain Waterpark, they had stopped to see this hill and paid the small fare to experience the effect of having their car "pulled" backwards up the hill by invisible, so-called magnetic forces. Aggie had been scared; Joanne had loved the uncanny effect—until she threw up. Their parents never took them back.

"I still don't know how that works," Bailey said.

"It's an illusion," said Alex.

"Care to explain it?"

Alex's face split into a smile and he chuckled; beneath them, the ground gave another low rumble and the sounds blended together. He frowned, down at the forest floor, momentarily lost in thought. "I guess I can't." He gazed around them and then remarked, "We've moved forward again."

The area they sat in was new. They were finally making ground. Bailey gave a groan of relief and flopped back on the moss behind him. Aggie could not even see their camp or where they'd danced anymore. A feeling like hope nosed around her stomach. She realised that she had, on some level, never believed they'd make it. Now, her mind was working overtime, portioning out their supplies like minutes to wages earned. Existence math: Lighter, three-quarters full, a thousand strikes. Half a liter of water, split between three adults—accounting for x-factor of unknowable kilometers walked, and variables of rain, puddles, etc.—sum payment, four days.

A person might, quite accurately, she thought, count the days of a life by such currency. What was currency, any currency, but an exchangeable form of time?

You couldn't buy more time, tack another seven hours onto the end of a week . . . but, in some ways, time was the *only* thing that could be bought. Collected by the pocketful, snared from the labour of others, their time to rattle around your belly like a nickel in a dented tin cup, something to keep you going for another day, another cool drink of a new morning. And when you didn't have anything else to trade for time, when you were too weary to earn your hour or there was no help left to gather more, you could watch your last minutes trickle away. It was a cold, cynical thought but Aggie had been on her own for a very long time, and cynical thinking—always preparing for the worst—had become a part of it.

She had tried to organize her life around that preparation. Always be prepared, never leave the house not ready for the worst. Because the worst, she knew, could happen simply by stepping out your own front door.

But now that a thing to be ready for had occurred, just one night testing her years of readiness, she wasn't so sure anymore. While she was glad to have a means of making fire, and water to drink, it all felt deeply anticlimactic and ultimately useless. Because she knew, deep down, those things would not have mattered were she out here on her own. She'd have more to eat and to drink, and for longer, but she was afraid she might have enjoyed it. The punishing test of her own mettle; to be so watchful and lonely. She would have tried to make herself proud, prove how long she could hack it. A sort of sick withholding. Pride was not a factor now, holding back not an option if they were to all survive. These were not the conditions by which she would have chosen their reunion, but she had to admit that she was glad to be with her brothers.

She had missed them.

Like he'd read her mind, Bailey said from his sprawl on the ground, "Might sound weird, but it's been good to spend time with you guys."

"We'll have to do it again sometime," agreed Alex.

A beat. Then belts of laughter. They saw each other laughing and then it was worse than ever. Bailey wheezed, "And again, and again, and again," and they all got going once more. They knew what was happening, pressure cooker laughter, the lid had been blown off, and that too added gas to the lunatic blaze. Their sides hurt by the time the gales had petered off to chuckles and sighs. Aggie wiped her cheeks; she had tears streaking her reddened face.

Bailey exhaled slowly, and then became very still, watching the swaying treetops and the hot summer sun above the shade.

They set camp as the sun went down on them for a second time. They were maybe ten feet from where they had been laughing.

There was no laughter now.

Aggie found herself eyeing a red squirrel that zipped across their camp and disappeared into the brush, wondering how to build a trap, imagining a fat little lump glistening on a spit, wondering if the meat would be sour. The water canister was down to a last swish at the bottom. The second lean-to did not come together as well as the first one—there was not as much usable brush in their immediate area—and they stayed by the fire longer just to keep warm. Shadows lay deep under their eyes; darkness pressed at their backs.

"I need to tell you guys something."

Bailey's voice was rough. The fire cracked and a mob of sparks hurried to the sky. The flames cut hard lines across his face.

"It's not forty grand I'm in for," he said. "It's twice that. At least, that's what the stuff we lost was worth."

Alex said, "What does that mean?" as Aggie sighed, "Oh, Bailey."

"It was a smaller debt before, but they said I could wipe it all out if I just carried this bag," Bailey went on dully, as though he had not heard them, as though he had to say this all at once or never. "I said, 'No problem,' but I get to the pick-up point and feel how heavy this bag is and I panic, a full out-of-body what-the-fuck-happened moment. There was another guy with me, no one really important but someone's nephew. Between sweating like I'd taken a dive in a swimming pool full of Crisco and nearly shitting myself, I think he figures me for a junkie. So, when I tell him I need to take a leak he's all too happy to get a little distance before our ride arrives. I duck into some bushes like a kid playing hide and seek. Well, someone must have been whispering in my ear because we had a tail. I'm hyperventilating behind the hedge of some old lady's lawn for maybe a minute before there are cops everywhere. I've never run so fast in my life, trying to outrun the bullet I was sure was five seconds away from getting lodged in my spine."

His eyes were very full, catching amber firelight, but his voice never wavered.

"I made it back to my apartment, grabbed my roommate's credit card and the tape, and got my ass to the airport where I bought a direct flight to Toronto. From there, I hitchhiked to Halifax. But I realized I couldn't stay with Dad. I'd have to explain. I lifted the wallet of the trucker who was giving me a ride when he was taking a piss and I used the cash to get a hostel until I could figure my shit out. I had been holding onto the tape, debating with myself whether to give it to the police or use it first, but now I was too afraid to go to the cops. Paranoid thinking to believe I was on some kind of international watchlist for a drug-bust nearly six-thousand kilometers away, but I didn't get where I was by thinking clearly, I guess, so . . . so, I figured I only had one option left. That the tape would be my lifeline. Somehow, I'd use it to get working again, pay off what I needed, make better connections . . . You were right, Alex, I wanted life rights from you two. I dragged you both into this. And now we're all here." He gave a dismal chuckle. "Can I comprehensively mess things up, or what? Holistically fucked."

Bailey was quiet for a long time. They let him have the silence. In the outside world, this story might have elicited admonishments of shock, dismay, and worried, bitter anger. But here in the woods, starving and cold, something as petty as a getaway from a one-time dope mule gig seemed somehow very inconsequential.

"I'm sorry," said Bailey at last. "For everything."

"It's going to be okay," said Aggie, but Bailey wouldn't have it.

"No, not just for what's happening now," he said. "But for what happened back then. With Joanne. It was my fault she left." He rubbed a hand over his mouth, eyes fire-fixed and far away. "It's always been my fault."

It had been a beautiful day with high winds in the trees, blue skies, and bumblebees drifting lazily from marigold to daisy to clover. The sea breeze coming out of the east had been light and good against their skin as the four siblings lazed or played in the July heat, skin dripping and sunscreen melting like vanilla ice-cream after an hour spent in their above-ground pool by the treeline in their backyard. Alex and Bailey were back in the pool. Alex ducked under the water—sound muffled, flat—knitting his hands to make a platform for Bailey to stand on as a fine stream of bubbles spilled from his lips. Bailey stepped on, gripping his big brother's shoulders, and then was flung, glistening and screaming overhead, sun heliographing off his skin as he plunged back into the raucous water. Alex shot back up again with a gasp, whipping his head, water spraying off the hair that he wore a just little long these days, in beads like sun-caught jewels.

Water slapped over the side of the pool, splattering Aggie's legs, the pages of her book, and dappling Joanne's bare belly as she lay on an old towel on the grass. Music squealed from Joanne's headphones. She gave no sign behind her mirrored aviators that she had noticed. Aggie looked up, lips bunching reproachfully.

"Watch it," she said.

"Don't sit so close to the pool," Alex said, smearing water

from his grinning face. Normally he didn't play this long with them anymore, getting older and cooler. There must have been something in the hot July sunshine.

"Again!" piped a struggling voice behind him. Bailey could only just touch the bottom, his neck had to be craned right back and his face right up to breathe. He danced on his toes, spinning small circles on the foamy, blue-marbled bottom. "Again!"

"I'm getting back in soon," said Aggie. "I just wanted to dry off." She screamed and snapped her book shut as Alex shot an open palm of water at her. She should have been mad, but she only felt giddy.

"Wet now," said Alex, laughing.

Aggie tossed her book aside, her feet smacking on the wet pool ladder as she scrambled up. With a roar, she launched herself at Alex, who feigned horror and dove under. They had a water fight, younger siblings against older; then boys against girl. They didn't team up older against youngest, it wouldn't have been fair.

"Jo, get in here," said Alex, loudly enough to be heard over the Rage Against the Machine blasting out of her Discman. Bailey was clinging to his back like a turtle shell, skinny legs around Alex's hips, freckled arms around his neck. Together they peered over the edge of the pool; Aggie stood on the ladder.

Joanne had turned over onto her stomach to sun the back of her legs, her face turned away on the nest of her folded arms. Aggie's lower jaw shivered, teeth rattling together as the water dried on her skin, raising little white goosebumps as they all waited for Joanne to say something. She had been like this for over a month, since graduating in June. She had barely scraped by, with some of her grades—they all knew—bumped up by sympathetic teachers who were proud of her swimming record. She was smart, really smart, Aggie thought, but she had never done well with school. Too much energy, the principal had told their parents at a meeting a few years back. Her lack of focus and unwillingness to "apply herself"—as she was dubiously diagnosed—was generally forgiven in light of her athletic prowess. And yet, like a worm at the core of a fine piece of fruit, worry nibbled at her parents. How long can a swimming career last, anyway? She could coach, but was that a real job? Did she want to do this her whole life? She'd figure it out as she went, Joanne would say. It was her life, just butt out. And so, while their parents would smile and nod and tell the whole world how proud they were, at home brochures for night schools and trade schools advertising professions she'd never shown the vaguest interest in appeared in the napkin basket in the kitchen or scattered around the living room. "Figuring it out" wouldn't cut it. Her parents were flashcard people about jobs, Aggie had thought one day as Joanne fought, again, with her parents and threw out the brochures. The only jobs they seemed to know or recognize could appear on a child's set of flashcards: D is for Doctor; F is for Firefighter; L is for Lawyer. They would never suggest W is for Waitress or C is for Cashier. Not even temporarily, not for their moderately famous daughter. But without the grades, what would she do next, what *could* she do that was serious? That would make them proud?

The sun baked their shoulders, the three in the pool and Joanne on her towel. At last, she sighed and pushed herself up onto her hands and knees. She turned off her Discman and stood, stretching her hands high over her head and arching her back slightly.

"I'm going to head inside and get a popsicle," she said.

Bailey squirmed on Alex's back. "Me too!" He crashed into the water and hopped for the ladder.

"Inside?" Alex sounded disgusted by the concept. "It's a perfect summer day, what are you going to do inside?"

"I don't know," she said, gathering her towel. "Mom and dad aren't home. Watch TV, play Nintendo, drink a beer."

"You can't have beer," Bailey said, scandalized, crawling

by Aggie on the ladder and then jumping down from the pool. He ran up to Joanne, water pouring off him and his blue trunks in big, ducky puddles. "You're only eighteen."

Joanne smiled. "You're right. You convinced me, I won't. Want that popsicle?"

Bailey perked like a little dog ready for a walk and held his hand up for her to hold.

"Oh, come on," said Alex, "we were having fun."

"Then keep having fun," said Joanne, turning away and walking with Bailey back to the house. "I'm not stopping you."

The breeze blew pine needles down from the trees; they lighted on the pool water without breaking the surface tension as Joanne pulled open the sliding patio door and disappeared into the cool dim of the house with Bailey.

"We could still play?" said Aggie, but without much hope or enthusiasm. The game was over. Alex said something about getting cold, anyway. He got out, towelled off, and went inside. Aggie found her book and pulled a lawn chair to a warm spot in the sun on the other side of the pool, out of the view of the house. Alex came back out, dressed in shorts, t-shirt, and sandals, and got his bike from where it lay by the dog run. He called to her to tell Joanne he'd gone to his friend David's house as he peddled off. He was up the driveway and gone before she could tell him to tell Joanne himself.

In the dog run, Doc started barking excitedly. Aggie got up from her chair and threw him a stick. He settled down in the shade of an overgrown lilac bush to happily chew it to splinters. She decided she wanted to take a walk. Without taking off her bathing suit, Aggie pulled on a pair of shorts and, telling no one, walked down their gravel driveway in her bare feet, crossed the pothole-pocked road, jumped over the mushy ditch, and strolled right into the woods.

It was a shortcut to the beach. The real way, the long way, would have taken her forty minutes on foot—down the rural road to an even *more* rural dirt road that led to the rocky shoreline. Aggie loved finding shortcuts, and she loved finding them with nothing but herself to carry, her hands snapping grey spruce branches out of the way, her toes feeling the invisible path beneath her feet, shaping a way that had never existed before through will and ingenuity. It made her feel good, it made her feel brave, like one of the lonesome, exploring heroines from the fantasy novels she devoured by the week. Brave and Alone. Things she could make all her own. Joanne had her swimming and was strong; Alex had his friends and was loyal; Bailey . . . well, Bailey was the youngest; he had everything. But Aggie knew how to be alone and how to be the fearless one out in the world.

She got to the rocky beach, feet stuck with pine gum and mud, and took in the view: The cold grey Atlantic, the endless stretches of evergreens and maple, and in the distance the high, rocky outcrop of the Cannon Park Nature Reserve. She thought she could hear the boom of the Caves, like a distant war drum, in the wind. The tide was nearly fully out.

Aggie took her time, building figures out of flat rocks, collecting shells, constructing little unlit campfires to be washed away later by the rising tide. When the water began to edge around her toes, having spent the afternoon creeping fifty meters up the shore towards her like a stalking cat, she decided it was time to head home. The sky was darkening to gold and violet and most of the heat of the sun was now trapped in the pink sunburn along her arms. It was warm to the touch, but she knew it wouldn't get too bad. Her hair was stiff with salt and wind, and she thought she might jump in the pool quickly to wash off before getting a huge glass of water.

She could hear the shouting before she was out of the woods. She ran the rest of the way home.

Her father was home, fighting with Joanne out in the yard. Bailey was sitting in the back of the family car, red face streaked with tears as he held his wrist; it curved at a funny angle.

"Could have drowned," said her father, storming around the car.

"I thought Aggie and Alex were out here with him," insisted Joanne. She looked scared, mad, hurt. She spotted Aggie coming up the driveway. She shouted, "Where were you?"

"The beach," she said. "What happened?"

"Aggie was alone, too?" snapped their father.

"I'm not a baby," Aggie said. "I go to the beach alone a lot."

But he would not be dissuaded from his anger. He jabbed a finger at his eldest. "Grounded, you hear me, Joanne?"

"Grounded?" Joanne laughed with anger. "I'm eighteen, you can't ground me."

"Watch me."

"No, watch me."

"By God, Joanne, while you live under my roof, you'll do as you're told!" He slammed the driver's door and shouted out his window as Alex walked his bike up the driveway. "That dog better be walked when I get home."

The car's tires spun a rooster tail of gravel. Doc jumped in his run, barking wildly, paws rattling the chicken wire door.

When the car was gone, Joanne rounded on Aggie. "Why did you wander off without saying anything? Where the hell were you?"

"Don't yell at her," said Alex, leaning his bike on the house. "What's going on?"

"Butt out."

"Did Bailey get hurt?" asked Aggie.

"I was taking a shower, he said he was going to go play in the pool," said Joanne. "I thought you two were still out here. He dove in, broke his wrist."

"He could have broken his neck, died."

"I know, Alex!"

"Hey!" he shouted. "Don't get mad at me."

70

"Well, I am mad at you!" she yelled, and the storm burst. "This whole fucking family is always coming down on me. I *was* here, I *was* watching him while you two just disappear. It's never your fucking fault!"

She turned to march back inside. Doc barked frantically at his run.

"You have to walk the dog," said Alex. He sounded mad and smug.

Joanne whirled on him. "Are you kidding me? You walk him."

"I've been playing soccer all day, I'm beat."

"I've been looking after our little brother all day."

"Not well enough," said Alex.

"You're a piece of shit."

"Dad said you do it," said Aggie, reasonably. "He'll just be mad if you don't."

Joanne smirked, the tip of her tongue zipping across her white teeth, disappointed with her little sister. The look hit Aggie like a wasp sting. Joanne went into the house. When she came out again, what felt like seconds later, she was wearing her windbreaker and carrying Doc's leash. She opened the gate and caught the dog by the collar, the big golden wiggling excitedly as she snapped the braided leash over his metal tag.

"Fuck this family," she said under her breath as she shouldered past them, down the driveway, and onto the road.

Aggie got her glass of water and finally got dressed. Alex made dinner and they ate in front of the TV. By nine, Alex started looking out the windows. At eleven, headlights flashed through the living room, and their father carried Bailey, wrist in a cast and fast asleep, up to his room. He told Aggie to go to sleep. After midnight, she could hear her father on the phone downstairs. "Hello, Mrs. Stewart? Sorry to call so late, is Joanne there?"

She woke to the smell of coffee brewing at four. At six, their father was in Alex's room telling him to watch the kids, he was going to drive around. At eight, Doc came trotting up the driveway, dopily panting, and dropped by the patio door after lapping water from his outdoor dish. Alex's friend called at ten, and Alex turned down the rematch soccer game and stayed on the couch between Aggie and Bailey, flicking through the channels to find cartoon after cartoon.

A police car pulled into the driveway around noon, followed closely by their father's car. The cops sat in the kitchen with their father, taking notes, and then asked to speak to the children one by one. The nice lady cop asked Aggie if she had seen anyone around yesterday, maybe someone in the woods? She had never thought before that someone might be in their woods.

Hours went by and they waited, eyes to the windows. Their mom came back from their Nana's, who she had been away helping, early. She ran into the house without seeing anyone until she saw their father and then started to cry. Aggie went to the front step and sat, listening to the crickets and watching the end of the driveway for Joanne to appear, hugging her knees and whispering, "Please, come back. Please, come back. I'm sorry. Please, please, please." She didn't know how to pray. She wanted to go looking by herself but was terrified to leave. Alex came out and put an arm around her.

Days went by.

Weeks.

The house became quiet while the whole world talked.

They waited, but their big sister never walked up the driveway again.

Joanne never came back.

"If I hadn't dived," Bailey said to the fire. "And there was a moment I knew I shouldn't. But I dove in anyway, thinking it would be fun."

"I could have told her where I was going, been there to watch you," said Aggie.

"Stop it." Alex's face was very red, even by the firelight. "I told her to walk the fucking dog after dad chewed her out. Kids aren't responsible, adults are. I'm a parent now, you know how often I've turned my back for a second, and found one of my kids running for the top of the stairs, or climbing cabinets, or—" He cleared his throat, but he would not look at them.

They'd never talked about that day together. Privately, they'd been repeating it for years, thinking of all the ways they might have changed things. It had changed all of them. They only shared lives with the people, the kids, they had been, and those lives were so different from the ones they might have lived if Joanne hadn't left that night. Would they have sat down that evening at dinner, Joanne telling a joke that would make them all laugh? Would their mother have called from their grandmother's house to wish them all good night? They would have fallen asleep, peacefully listening to the crickets and the distant rumble of the Caves, not knowing what calamity had been avoided. In September, the family would have cheered Joanne on, never a doubt in their minds that she would take home gold, that she would stand high on her podium and wave to the world. A whole world of experience and memory burnt away like an overheated movie reel.

Aggie got to her feet. "We should sleep." Her tone was short, and she didn't know why.

Once again, they wriggled into position under the lean-to, sparse as it was, and sought out sleep.

Once again, Aggie awoke before morning and saw the woman by the dying fire. She stood in profile tonight, eyes round, white, mad, and grinning. When Aggie saw her face, she bit her hand until it bled to keep from screaming.

In the morning, Aggie said nothing. She had not fallen back to sleep after the woman left, could not, and knew it wasn't a dream. She didn't tell her brothers what she'd seen; she didn't want them to think she was losing her mind. There was nothing to eat and she let them talk over what to do about the last of the water as she stared watchfully into the trees. After agreeing they would not drink the last of the water until they absolutely had to, they moved on. Soon thirst and fatigue consumed all Aggie's thoughts and she stopped looking for the woman.

Hours passed. Aggie's head felt tight, her whole body ached. It was hard to keep her chin level to the ground as they walked. Step after step after step towards nothing.

Bailey fell just before noon. Aggie heard the crash and groan behind her.

"I'm okay," he grunted, as she helped him up. "Blister just popped. I tripped." He favoured the right side, hopping a little as he stood and grimaced.

"Would it be better to walk in bare feet?" she asked.

"Maybe." He sniffed, pride not kicking him down yet, and looked around. His pained face became a measure more anxious. "Where's Alex?"

"Over here."

Alex was standing a good fifty meters away. The lopsided grin splitting his grimy, unshaved face melted away years. He almost looked like a teenager again.

"Don't wander off!" Aggie shouted. "We could get separated."

"I think I figured it out," he said, too excited to pay any mind. "We're still in sight of one another, and I think that matters. Just wait where you are, and I'll tell you when to come forward."

He crouched down and put his hands to the ground, cocking his head to one side like a cowboy in an old western sussing out the thundering approach of cavalry. After a minute of steely concentration, his face lit and he looked up. "Walk towards me, now."

They did. After ten seconds or so he commanded, "Stop! Wait." In a few minutes, he told them to go again.

It took several attempts but at last they were side by side once more. Bailey and Aggie looked around cautiously.

"We're not in the same spot," said Aggie, wondering.

"I figured it out," Alex told them. "When a big wave goes by, when you can feel one of the tremors, the loop stops. You can move forward unaffected."

"The vibrations must blank out the stone tape momentarily," said Bailey. "Stop the record. Well fucking done, man."

"I don't care what it is or what it's doing," said Alex, impatiently, as though the grounded, skeptical part of him—despite their lived experience—was embarrassed to even indulge such theories. "Point is, we don't have to be wasting energy and time. We can pace ourselves, not lose ground by walking at the wrong times."

Aggie felt her pulse quicken, felt almost breathless. "Then let's keep putting it to the test."

They continued in this measured, halting fashion. They would move only when they could feel the tremors, then they would stop and Alex, who turned out to be the most adept at detecting even the smallest vibrations, would crouch once more to feel out the next wave. Sometimes they were lucky and the waves came in rapid succession. But as the afternoon wore on, the tremors became less frequent. The ground rose under them and became thicker, stonier. Vibrations were harder to detect through the network of glacial boulders and settled rock beneath their feet, and when they did pick a tremor up, it was fainter, shorter. Their windows of advancement became tighter and sometimes they could only get a few steps before it would close again.

"Tide must be going out," said Alex. His hand curled into a fist over the ground he'd been testing for over half an hour. He threw a cold clod of dirt and needles irritably into the trees. "The waves aren't as strong."

They had looped twice, Aggie thought.

"Three times," Bailey said. She hadn't realized that she'd

said anything, and she looked at him, surprised. Bailey lowered his voice so only she could hear as Alex muttered and paced like a big cat in a cage. "And we've already had this conversation. It's getting late," he called to Alex as Aggie felt suddenly very dizzy, "We should pitch camp."

"Too early," said Alex.

"It will be dark in a few hours," said Bailey. "We don't want to set up in the dark."

"We don't have to spend another night here," insisted Alex, patrolling his patch of ground and occasionally stamping his foot, like he might flush out more readable ground.

Aggie was still staring at Bailey. "Did I say something?"

"Yes," said Bailey, quietly. "And you've asked that question, too. You're just tired. We can't be far." He took her hand and smiled. "It'll be okay. Al, come give it a break."

Alex stopped his pacing, fixed a frustrated glare on them—and was gone.

Aggie and Bailey shouted in surprise at the empty space where their brother had been. Aggie's brain caught up with her eyes and she ran forward, calling his name. There came a groan in reply. Aggie slid to a stop, approaching the spot carefully. Up close, she could see there was a hole, a tattered break in the earth roughly the width and length of a large coffin. Ragged leaves hung over the side like the wrinkled lips of a toothless old woman's mouth. She and Bailey crawled to the edge, peering over. Aggie raised her arm to bar Bailey's chest, saying in a hushed voice, "Careful."

Alex turned his face up, white with shock and streaked with mud, from some twelve feet below.

"Are you okay?" said Aggie.

Alex nodded uncertainly. He moved his legs, starting with his ankles, and experimentally got to his feet. He slipped an inch, and he quickly pressed his back to the rock wall behind him. His face shot up. He looked scared, but he sounded calm. "I don't think this is the bottom."

They saw what he meant. A small, black hole had opened at the other end of the narrow pit. As they watched, another fist-sized chunk of dirt dropped soundlessly away into the blackness below. Bailey sat straight up.

"Hold tight, we'll find a way to get you up!"

Alex shook his head. "I don't think you can."

There was another tremor, louder than they had ever been. It echoed up through the shifted earth, coming clear through the deeper pit.

"Right where you're standing, are you on solid ground?" said Aggie. Alex shifted one foot. The hole at the other end widened again by a few chocolaty crumbs as the tremor subsided.

"Seems like. For now."

"We're going to get you out."

"Aggie?"

"Just stay very still."

"Aggie," said Alex, very clearly. "You've been trying for an hour."

Scattered around the top of the hole were broken alder branches, some half woven together into failed ropes before they splintered and broke. There were no branches big enough to climb and none small enough to braid a rope. Bailey turned his hands over: they were bleeding from pulling down branches. Aggie was holding her knife but had no memory of taking it out. Alex let the understanding wash over them.

"You can't stay here," he told them. "Staying in one spot, the longer you're here, it's making it worse. Please, don't make me tell you again.

"Your only choice," Alex went on as they began to argue, "is to go."

"We'll come back with help, ok Alex?" said Aggie. "You just hold tight."

Bailey looked at her like she was nuts.

Alex smiled, sadly. "No coming back."

Aggie stared down furiously at him. He shook his head. "I'm sorry, Aggie."

LAURA KEATING

Getting to her feet felt like the hardest thing she'd ever
done, but when she stood, she was steady. Bailey stared up
at her, confounded.

"We're not leaving," he said.

"You've been out-voted," said Alex.

"That's bullshit. There is no vote."

"We have to go," said Aggie, taking his arm. Bailey
slapped her hand away.

"Fuck no we don't," he said. "We have to keep trying.
We'll be fine, you're not looping."

"I don't have any other options," said Alex. "No do overs."

"It's not over."

"Bailey," Aggie said.

"I'm not going!"

"Look at me."

He glared up at her and then hung his head. He started
to cry. He knew what she would say, and she was right. They
had been trying. If they stayed, eventually they'd loop until
they couldn't stop. None of them would make it. Aggie took
her backpack off, considered it for a second, with its last bit
of water and her poncho, and then dropped it down into the
pit. Alex caught it. He held it to his chest.

"I can hear the water below," he told her. "It's coming
back strong. You'll have another opening soon." He raised
one hand in farewell. Aggie thought if she opened her mouth
she'd be sick and then she'd lose her nerve. She nodded once
and moved away from the pit edge.

Bailey stayed longer, trying to talk him out of a situation
that would not yield to either words or will. He spoke to his
brother like it was the last time he would ever see him. Which
it was. And when he finally joined Aggie, he was sobbing. He
stumbled into her as the next tremor began and she took his
hand, pulling him, stiff-armed, along behind as he buried his
face in his other arm, the trees swallowing them whole as the
world shifted for a moment like sliding glass doors. And they
moved on.

VII
WHAT AGGIE SAW

THE SUN FELL in the sky, and they pressed on.

Aggie and Bailey took turns sensing out the tremors. They were harder to detect, and the going was slower than ever. Bailey had been dropping items along the way. Aggie did not try to dissuade him from his breadcrumb trail. It was something he had to do, to feel like he was doing something. He purged his sunglasses, cards from his wallet, his cellphone. He tied torn pieces of his scarf to trees, and when that was done, he ripped the sleeves from his t-shirt. Aggie had to stop him from leaving his jacket. "Won't be much good if you get hypothermia," she warned him.

They were both starving and thirsty beyond reckoning. Aggie's mouth felt like it had been packed with cotton, her throat burned. Her head swam from exhaustion, was tight with headache, and she'd developed a faint ringing in her ears like a struck tuning fork. Her feet began to drag as the sun went down. Bailey was badly limping now, his feet in torment. Aggie could see blood on the back of his calves, soaking through his jeans where the edge of his low boots had chafed away the skin. They had to take more frequent breaks, skipping some of the tremors, and when it got dark Aggie got out her cellphone and turned on the flashlight. The screen flashed static as Alex's had. The lush, dense woods was transmuted by the cold diode of the flashlight to flat silvers and blacks. She was unable to see further than a cold circle of trees at any given time. They pressed on in the dark. Aggie was determined not to think about how dark the pit would be now, about the expanding darkness on the other end.

The trees stared down at them, a repeating ring of cruel judges, their trunks pulling closer and tighter on them like the contracting iris of a glaring eye. It was her turn to feel for a wave, but when she sat down she ended up laying down and there curled her knees to her chest, stomach cramping, hands clasped under her chin like huddled doves. Bailey laid down beside her and used his jacket to cover them both. They slept like they had as children, on those nights when Joanne would come home late and she and their mother would fight, uneasy but safe with each other.

"*Hey.*"

She did not know how long she had been asleep, but it was still dark when Aggie opened her eyes. She was momentarily blinded by the light of the phone, needles shooting straight from her eyes to her brain. She had not turned the flashlight off. Aggie turned her head, almost imperceptibly, to look over her shoulder at Bailey but she could see he was asleep and dreaming. They did not look like good dreams, but he needed rest and she did not wake him.

"*Hey.*"

The voice came again. She looked around into the woods but could not see past the light into the dark. Fear coiled in her. Too afraid to turn the light off, too afraid to shine it out into the trees, she remained motionless. She remembered the figure at their campfire. That first night, she had thought it might be Lynn; the second night she had seen otherwise. Aggie pretended like she hadn't heard the whisper, and through half-closed eyes she raked her gaze around the woods.

She could see a little deeper into the trees as she grew accustomed to the dark, and then she saw it. The face in the dark.

It was her own.

The pale of her filthy forehead, the spread of her grinning mouth, the wide, staring eyes were all she could see. All else was darkness and night. The figure, the face, stood amongst the trees. It was not looking right at them but somewhere about two feet above. It, she, couldn't quite see them, but she knew or at least suspected they were there.

Bailey whimpered in her ear, and Aggie willed him to stay asleep, to be quiet.

The Herself in the woods was still carrying a backpack. The pack looked fuller. There were no versions of Alex or Bailey nearby, at least not that she could see. Aggie remembered its darkened hands. She had thought it was dirt.

Was this the "her" that Bailey had seen when Duke broke his leg, who went off for help but never came back? Or was this a dream, she thought. Just a starved, dehydrated, exhausted dream. If it was a dream, it was a vivid one, complete with hunger pangs, cold moss pillows, the itch of sweat, insects, and broken blisters.

Leave him.

This had not come from the woods but from inside her own head. Still, it sounded as clearly as words spoken. The dark and the night had become a filter and through it her thoughts were distilled; things she would not think by day became enunciated and clear. Here, in the night, she could admit that she *was* mad at Bailey, that she had *always* been mad. Had always blamed him as much as herself. He was irresponsible, the reason Joanne was gone, the reason they were here, the reason they were slowing down. He was pathetic and selfish.

The grin in the woods widened.

Even when he messed up, he was comforted and coddled, had always gotten away with it, whatever "it" was—including his biggest mess-up of all. He was the reason their sister was gone. And still everyone had gone to him, asked him questions, made sure that he was safe while Aggie had to be strong, for him and for everyone else, because there wasn't enough warm comfort to go around. They had to think someone was okay, and the weight of her own strength had crushed her, made her small. She had fed parts of herself to the forge that had always burned so hot within her, building her armor until her forge choked and faltered, and with nothing left to burn she'd retreated, walled herself off and forgot what was beyond those walls. It was a burning, cold comfort that lit in her now, to have someone to hate. Anger was an easier emotion to process than fear or sadness. It allowed her to think. Here, she was trapped. But once, and maybe still out there, in the dark, she was the girl who wandered.

If she left, would this other take her spot? Would they pass each other, shoulder to shoulder, not a word spoken? She could go on tonight, maybe find her way out, never worry about this other, her brothers, or anyone else ever again. She could wander off, say nothing, carrying nothing.

A sound, not from in front of her but behind.

Bailey.

The face in the dark became a fraction displeased. Aggie was beginning to think of It less as herself, though they shared a face. Bailey whispered her name, voice tight, a thread of wind seeking entrance against an unstable home. At once, leaving became unthinkable. He had just been an easy person to blame, the littlest and Joanne no longer around to defend him. The face in the woods—

Leave him.

—watched . . . and Aggie grabbed her brother.

"Hey, wake up."

Aggie opened her eyes.

Bailey was sitting up next to her, one hand on her shoulder as he rustled her awake. "Wake up," he repeated.

Aggie looked around, confused. "You were having a nightmare."

He shrugged. "You were the one still asleep."

Aggie sat up and peered into the trees. The sky was wash-water grey; they were maybe an hour to sunrise. The face in the woods was gone. Either it never was, or it had moved on to some place between, she couldn't say.

Bailey sat back on his heels, wincing slightly. Clearly hurting, but his gaze was steady. She did not like the way he stared at her.

"You were talking in your sleep," said Bailey.

"I dreamed you were." Her voice was dry and hoarse. The night had become very cold. The night creatures had settled, and the dawn chorus refused to rise. "What did I say?"

For a moment, it looked like Bailey would not tell her. But after consideration, he said, "Leave him."

She didn't deny it.

"You think you'd have a better chance of getting out without me?"

She thought about lying, but only for a second. "Yes. But I won't."

He nodded, thoughtfully, and then looked away into the dark, back the way they'd come.

"You know," he said, "everyone in this family is always looking out for me. At least, that's what you tell yourself you're doing. But you only do it so you can keep feeling hurt, like you deserve to be hurt, while also telling yourself you're doing something noble. Protection and punishment, rolled into one. I don't need protection, Aggie." He set a hard look on her. "And you don't need punishment."

"It's not like that."

"You're doing it again," he said. "Stop protecting me. You can feel angry. I'm angry." He pointed, almost lazily, to their right. "There's the trail."

She followed where he was pointing and saw that he was right. It was the end of the muddy trail she and Alex had first come by. They had come upon it last night and not even noticed.

There was another tremor almost immediately. Deep in

the woods, there was a thunderous crack, like a tree coming down. Bailey left his jacket. With nothing to carry, they got themselves up and headed onto the path.

Bailey took the lead. Limping badly, he held onto the small trees on either side of the trail to pull himself along. The tremors never seemed to stop now, not entirely, but this worried Aggie rather than encouraged her.

At last, the shaking stopped, and they had to stop to rest. It did not seem to be getting any brighter. Aggie didn't know if that was because of heavy cloud cover above the trees, or if the influence of the magnetism, whatever it was, was spreading out and up as the ground broke apart. They waited. Over an hour and then more. There were deep growls from down below, more cracks of falling trees, but not enough, and when they tried to move forward, they found themselves retracing their own muddy footprints over and over.

They didn't speak. They barely even looked at one another.

Bailey sat right down on the ground, elbows on his knees, agitatedly running his hands through his hair. Aggie thought she hadn't really looked at her little brother in years. At the cafe, she'd thought she'd hated him . . . but why? He had been standoffish, but hadn't *she* hung up on *him*, over and over, for years, barely willing to hear him out? Did she resent the life he had or simply that it had been offered to him when it had never been offered to her? That he had still tried where she had given up? Or did she, on some level, know that she had helped to dress him in this lifestyle, piece by piece? Every time she said she was okay, every time she hid, every time she told the world how to treat her and told herself she didn't want anything in return. She had done that. She'd been pretending to be resilient, and had decided that by accepting help her brother was weak.

But now she could see he had only been trying to play a part as surely as she had, and that the bravado, the show, it had all been proof of purchase, what her mother's coddling had bought, and she and Alex had wrapped up safe. Then together, they had congratulated themselves with one face for the good job they had done keeping a little boy from reality, while with another face had resented him for being out of touch. But reality had been there all along and just like she had hidden, tried to disappear, to not be a burden, he had tried to shine for them and to fix it in the only ways that a guilt-ridden and sheltered little boy knew how. He was not entirely blameless, no one was ever entirely blameless for the lives they lead, and he was not without his own provocations . . . but in the end, all he'd ever wanted, like the rest of them, was to grieve and be forgiven.

It was hard to grieve for a missing person, when hope kept insisting they were alive. He'd said he was angry, and what was anger but one of the many facets of grief? After the shock, pain, and guilt came the grief. Without closure, they had all become mired in it. She had hidden, walled herself away from the world. Alex had given up his carefree ways, become focus-hardened, all sacrificing. And Bailey had tried to outshine it all, a blinding light of ambition through which all the pain of the past might be erased. But it had erased nothing, time had taken everything, and still they'd held onto their precious pain.

She'd let herself believe that grief was the deepest expression of love, but grief was not love any more than memory was the sum of a life. It was the final cry out for apology to the life unlived, and only forgiveness could set them right again.

As she watched her brother, the anger she'd kept so protected, so hidden that she had forgotten it was there, flared and started evaporating like rain on hot steel.

"Bailey," she said, but there was another clear rumble, louder than anything they'd heard before. Bailey got up and was moving again. She followed, knowing that they had to be near the end. The shaking didn't stop. The trail grew brighter as the trees thinned. Mud sucked at their feet, needles shivered and fell all around like confetti. She stumbled, and Bailey took her hand. They had arrived at the end of the path, and they stepped out together.

The path was gone.

But she was there.

VIII
LODESTONE

THEY STARED IN dumb wonder. The landscape, so rent and twisted, was hard for their exhausted minds to comprehend. Where there had once been forest and the service road, a huge sinkhole the size of a stadium had opened up, falling away into the ocean. Salt water had rushed to fill the chasm, the toppled rocks of the landslide had plowed great swaths of land up the other side like huge grasping fingers. The waves below crashed and sent white sprays of saltwater hundreds of feet into the air. Sea birds screamed and dove into the mist. Trees leaned; wood and bark had exploded, torn asunder or turned upside down, their roots kicked up in the air, pulling the land up in huge hoary nets of clay and stone.

They stood gazing in awe and shock at the cataclysmic damage, but also at the trail: even, quiet, and sane. And upon it walked Joanne.

They could hear the gravel softly crunching under her sneakers. They could smell the pine in the night air. Joanne took three steps towards them and then turned back, leash in hand, calling for Doc.

"Doc? Here boy!" Her voice was clear. And then she was gone.

Back again in its entirety was the shifted rock as it slid and cascaded into the watery crater, sloshing with the freezing tide.

Both things were true. The now and the then. The crater and the path. They stood at the lip of ruin and she walked in peace. How and why it happened, and why still the moment played, they would never know. Whether she was the lodestone or just another needle drawn in agony to its gravity was beyond either their knowledge or understanding, but it did not require their understanding to be true. It was an unforgiving landscape.

Through the blurring air, their sister arrived, looked about, and lost her way again, as unaware of her suspended predicament as a leaf tossed in a hurricane.

Or at least, that was what Aggie hoped.

The ground beneath their feet was not safe. More rock and mud rolled from the edge into the water below. Aggie could see no way forward. There was a tug behind her navel, a pull like an invisible hand had wrapped around her spine and was drawing her onwards. The pull was becoming strong. She watched as trees flickered, grew, shrank to saplings, fell, and rotted only to once more grow tall and strong. All moments, every moment, all at once and flashing before them like great shutters opening and closing on the wind. Joanne was there and then gone. It was twenty years ago, it was now, it was unknown years later. All of this and none of this was happening; the world as she saw it and the world as it was drawing and repelling, shifting in unstable beats.

She was only just aware of Bailey's lips grazing her cheek a moment before he let go of her hand. She hesitated—and too late she tried to grab him back.

The cliff crumbled and Aggie jumped backwards just as the path rose up under Bailey's feet and he walked out on it and towards Joanne.

Their sister stood under the flickering lamppost, moving an eternally falling strand of hair from her face. A sound over her shoulder caught her attention. Joanne turned around. The worry in her eyes was real but it eased the moment she saw the young man limping towards her. Aggie could see that she knew him. He was older, taller than her now, but it made no difference. Joanne hesitated, then went to him like she had been expecting him, hoping. She opened her arms.

For a horrifying moment, Aggie thought this had to be a trick, that it was not Joanne, nor had it ever been. This person was an illusion or a monster who would now unhinge her jaw and reveal a mouth of lion's teeth.

But she did not because she was not a monster. She was their sister. Joanne wrapped her brother in her arms, and he pulled her close, resting his head on her shoulder without fear or hesitation.

He was on her side. He always had been.

And then they were gone.

IX
WAY BACK

THE CLOUDS WERE breaking up, the storm Aggie had feared had come to nothing. The sky was a patchwork of blue and grey, and the birds were beginning to sing again. She sat. She waited for a very long time for them to come back, to reappear and step out on this side of twenty years together. But they never did. The path did not reappear. Whatever draw, whatever charge this place had, though shattered and weakened with the collapsing ground, it still had power; but that door was closed. As she sat on the ground, staring, trees around her flickered and disappeared. Some flared and burned out. Maybe some were only the ghosts of trees, had been for years. How would she or anyone else ever know the difference? But she wasn't really thinking of that. All she could think of was *Alone*.

For years she had cut herself off. She would sometimes go weeks without seeing anyone, even in a small town, but in those weeks Alex would always call and eventually come by. She could check Bailey's social media and see how happy he was. In this fashion, she had told herself for years that she was resilient, steady, and that they were the ones who fretted or who filled their world with distractions.

She willed them to come back, all of them, as the stone tapes fought to replay and to make order again in the broken world. But the world would not recycle just because she wanted it to. The clock wasn't meant to run backwards, the sand to eternally fall. It moved on.

The world still felt like it was bending around her. Her head pounded, and it took her a long time to understand what she was hearing.

A helicopter.

The thump of its twin rotor blades faded in and out as it circled. Her mud- and sweat-smeared face tipped up, neck and stiff shoulders raging. She scanned the breaking blue sky but could not see it yet—which of course meant they could not see her.

Scale the stones, a voice told her.

If she got higher, she might be able to flag help. She got unsteadily to her feet as there came another crash in the trees, the loops still taking place behind her where there was still ground for it to grind.

Get higher, the voice told her.

Her legs held, but only just. Her bones felt like they were made of sand. She felt very cold, and she considered that on top of hunger and exhaustion she was probably in shock. She knew she was, in fact, by the way her eyes kept roving to the place where Bailey had stepped away from her side and out of her reality. She needed something new to fix her eyes and mind upon.

Go. It was a good, solid word. *Out.*

She could not fixate on just the first step, but all the potential ones ahead. She could not sit in a theatre without looking for the exits, and from those exits know what street she was stepping out onto. It was an anxious, taxing way of living but it had felt like survival, and this well-worn programming kicked in now.

In her mind it was already done: how she would climb and sidle around the edge of the sinkhole to the top of the rock pile nearest her right. The stones would be cold and slick, so recently birthed from aeons underground, and she would need to take great care in reaching the top. Within a minute of reaching the crest of the mound, a red helicopter would see her waving her leaden arms, her face banded with dirt, and a man in a yellow jumpsuit would be lowered down with a harness. She would be hoisted up and, rocked by the motion of the chopper, fall asleep, despite the noise, despite everything. She would sleep and wake at the hospital to be told by a nurse with clean hands and a full schedule that her parents had been contacted, and asked was there anyone else they needed to call? She would tell them there was not.

There was no one.

Alex had never left her alone; in all the years she had tried to isolate herself. He'd checked in on her, made sure she was all right, picked her up when she was spiraling. Bailey was never going to leave Joanne alone; he would have looked for her forever. She could not reach them now, that moment was cut off forever, but behind her there was still a chance. The way home was the way back.

She did not see if the helicopter rounded the bend.

She plunged back into the trees and followed the trail Bailey had left, a clearer and more stable path than any one they had been following for days. She could not follow the tremors anymore, they were too inconsistent, both in frequency and power. Whatever that mechanism was, it was failing and fast. Like a compass needle, it only pointed one way.

She did not loop often, either because she had been this way before or because she had new markers to direct her on a trail already blazed. Or perhaps it was that she already knew where she was going, her mind fixed on that dark point like a beacon. When she did loop, it was because she had strayed from the trail or had hesitated before seeking out the next marker. The going was faster, geographically they had never gone far.

And she was not alone.

They came in first as voices, distant as an old radio broadcast. Then they passed her as ghosts. More than once she passed Bailey and herself, still and forever desperately trying for the way out. Each time they passed one another, the self she had been would shiver and Bailey would look around as though alert to a strange sound . . . and he'd tie a new marker on a tree.

She arrived at their camp. Together they lay on the ground, but only she was asleep, crying and asleep. Bailey sat up, worry on his face, and then he saw her. The sun had risen on her, but he had to stare from the dark. He did not startle but looked down again at the sleeping Aggie next to him.

"I never would have left you," she told him. "But I understand why you had to go."

He did not look at her again, but spoke to her sleeping self, "I'm sorry, Aggie." She wanted to go to him, to hold him one more time, but when she took another step, they were gone. She kept moving forward.

She was being followed.

She could see her hideous self, crouched and crawling through the woods, gone mad, feasting on some animal, her hideous self who only hid and hated. That self did not see her and she moved on quickly. There were more great growling crashes as the chasm spread, the ocean pawing at the sheer walls, and the ground collapsed behind her.

It was maddening how little time it took to find the pit.

"*Alex*?" Her voice was a whisper, wilted by thirst and the fear that she was too late. She forced herself closer, carefully edging forward, and cleared her throat. "Alex?"

The silence from the black gash was deafening. Then: "Aggie?"

She hastily crawled the rest of the way over. The ground felt unreal, shifting beneath her hands like a blanket covering the rotted floorboards of a derelict house. She gripped the edge of the pit and looked down.

Alex's pale, drained face stared back up. The floor of the pit was almost entirely gone, standing room only. The blackness below roiled with unearthly sounds. The last of the

Cannon Caves, not yet collapsed, roared like a wounded animal.

All around her shades of herself and Bailey flickered and sparked, stripping branches and failing to twist them into secure ropes.

"Where's Bailey?" said Alex.

The answer would not come. She promised if they made it out, she would try to explain.

"The ground isn't safe to walk on," she said. "Everything is breaking apart." Even in saying so, she watched a tree to her left sink, straight down into the earth like a pencil chewed up by a giant sharpener. She lined her body parallel to the hole and carefully threw a leg over the side.

Alex realised what she was doing too late.

"Aggie, stop!"

Her sneakers hit the ground hard, and she toppled forward into a crouch, nearly going ass over heels into the deeper pit. Alex grabbed her shirt before she could tumble headlong into the dark and yanked her back.

The steady, vibrating growl within the walls of the earth was maddening. Worms and beetles wriggled out of the mud walls and dropped to the floor in a frantic attempt to escape the pulsations. Alex took Aggie by her shoulders, almost shaking her.

"I told you not to come back." But the fury in his eyes was surface thin; beneath there was terror and helplessness. Aggie wasted no time. Her backpack was at his feet, nearer the wall. She brushed several worms from it and loosened the damp waist strap to its fullest extent. Then she looped the shoulder straps over Alex's arms. He did so compliantly, watching her with the detached calm of a child having their shoe tied.

"You're bigger, so you'll have to hold onto me," she told him and stepped up so there was no space between them. He was taller and his hips were at her waist. She clipped the bag's hip straps around her back and cinched them as tightly as she could. She tugged the nylon strap one last time. "We're going to jump."

94

Alex's mouth came open, his haze lifting momentarily.

"It's like the old camp song," said Aggie, interrupting him before he could argue. "Can't go over it, can't go around it. Got to go through it."

There was water down below, they could both hear it: The rush like a cosmic vacuum, the boom, and that gargling slurp of the water pulling back into the ocean. Another chunk of ground fell away as a wave boomed underground. Aggie wiped her sweating palms on her jeans. She had no idea how far down the water was, or if they'd even survive the fall. They had to time it just right.

Too soon and they'd be crushed by the wave, spun around and smeared across the cave. Too late, they could hit bare rock at the bottom, shatter their legs and skulls.

Alex wrapped his arms around her whole body, gripped her tight. Aggie hugged his middle, tucked her head to his chest and nodded.

"One," she began to count. But the water came in faster, stronger than it had before, and they jumped to meet the full, swollen crest.

Darkness, falling forever, trying to take a deep breath— then plunging into freezing water.

The water was mind-stoppingly cold. Aggie was out and then, regaining her senses, she sucked in a panicked lungful of water. She was briefly aware of a tremendous, cavernous space, centuries hollowed out, a cathedral carved out of the stone. She felt small, embryonically small. Then the wave pressed down on them with a mountain of pressure as the suction pulled them back toward the sea.

Alex's fingers gripped her arms so tight she thought he might rip the frozen meat right from her bones. The rushing water wrenched her right arm free from her grip around his back and it fluttered in the accelerating current like a hurricane-striped flag. Her whipping hair snagged; a chunk ripped from her scalp. There was stinging pain, numbed by the cold, but then her erratic arm smashed into a rock wall, snapping her wrist sideways and dragging the thin part of her hand against the ragged stones until it was pulp. The last of her air burst from her chest in a scream of black bubbles. She felt herself slip an inch in the straps, more. And then brightness. They were tumbling, over and over, as the rushing subsided, relaxed to a swift but steady current. Alex released her with one arm, and she was distantly aware that he was kicking. She wanted to kick too but couldn't get her legs to work as she slumped ever lower in the harness. Grey nothingness ate at her vision like brewing storm clouds.

Sound came back all at once. A burst of gulls crying, waves splashing, Alex huffing then coughing in her ear. Sight was more reluctant to return. She could only see in tones of grey and white. Another, smaller wave pushed them like a playful friend. Further out to sea or toward land, she did not know. Pain stung her bleeding head like tiny needles, the wind skipping across the water tapped her numb face. She coughed, warm salty water flooding over her blue lips and she gasped in the air. Alex said something she couldn't make out, and when she looked up again, she saw she had been turned around in the harness, her back now to his chest. He was making for shore, towing her with both arms hooked under her armpits, his hands supporting the sides of her head. Her arms floated out and in front of her, listless, like they belonged to someone else. Her right wrist lay flat against her forearm, limp as a shot bird. Half of her right hand was missing. Her pinky had been stripped entirely away, the torn skin unzipping halfway to her elbow. A splintered white spike swaddled in pink and white flesh was all that remained of her ring finger. The blood in the water was dark and she was losing a lot of it. Dimly, she raised it out of the water, to her chest, and squeezed below her shattered wrist. Her eyes rolled skywards to the blue above. Seagulls screamed against the wind. A thudding beat, like a distressed heart, grew steadily closer.

"She could only see in tones of grey and white. Another smaller wave pushed them...further out to sea, or toward land, she did not know."

X
START AGAIN

THE FLOOR FAN ruffled the pages on the desk.

It had all happened much like she imagined it would.

The helicopter had landed up the shore, scaring a group of seals diving into the water. Aggie had been wrapped in a blanket, loaded onto a stretcher, and hurried back onboard. The rocking of the machine had lulled her into a deep and dreamless sleep—but not before she saw, from high above the trees, a quarter of the park slide off into the ocean, sending up a wave that momentarily cleared the ocean floor. Her hospital room had been bright and a nurse with clean hands and a full schedule informed her that her parents had been contacted.

Her brother had given them the details.

She moved some of the papers from her desk with one hand, began to go through them . . . and then simply dropped the lot into one of the black garbage bags plopped around her apartment. The slim claw of her bandaged right hand was strapped to her chest in a tight sling. They had been able to reset her wrist, but it would be months before she could sit effectively at a computer for any length of time. Even then, she would have to completely relearn how to type.

The side door opened. Alex walked into the kitchen with another armload of empty boxes and placed them on the floor. There was a lot of space to move around now; the table and chairs had already been sold to a pair of students who would be attending the local community college that fall, and all the dishes, cutlery, and pots and pans had been packed up and donated. Everything else had found its way into the dumpster out back. She hadn't been able to watch at first, had locked herself in her room and even cried. But slowly, very slowly, she'd begun taking things apart on her own, keeping those things she loved and parting with those things she no longer needed. There was not much she loved. There had been bad moments, there had been regrets, there had been pleas to put it all back, but in the end the call was hers, and in the end she kept going. Along with the kitchen, most of her living room was cleared; only the desk and its surrounding atmosphere retained the sedimentary layers she had placed there, year after year. The furniture remained, but soon it too would be sold.

Alex straightened up and stretched his back. "Want me to get started in the bedroom?"

The stitches over his left eyebrow were already beginning to work themselves out and dissolve. In another week, he'd be left with a short scar. He'd been lucky, barely scraping the rocks and barnacles, and had only spent two days in the hospital for treatment of shock and exposure. Margot and the kids had been able to talk to him a mere hour after he was admitted. Aggie had been sedated prior to arrival and the surgery on her hand. She had blurry memories of Alex limping into her room to see her, looking far too big for the blue hospital shirt and robe they had stuffed him into.

"How are you feeling?" he had asked then. Aggie looked at him, then down to the missing part of her hand.

"Like it was a fair exchange."

She was discharged on the fifth day and went home with Alex and Margot. They had been settling her into their guest room when the police arrived. They, of course, asked about Bailey. He and the film crew were not the only people missing. Aggie and Alex filled them in on the events from their end. They had confirmed their story on the drive home from the hospital. It was very simple.

"We went to the park when Bailey told us he had a lead on our missing sister," said Aggie. "His former production had caught the same lead."

"Were the police notified?"

Alex shrugged. "You tell me."

They explained how they had doubted but indulged him. They had met the two members of the location crew and set off toward a disused trail in an out-of-bounds section of the park when a sinkhole had opened up. Alex and Aggie had been separated from the others. They had been trapped until another tremor from the landslides had broken through a cavern below.

"Sounds like you were very lucky."

Neither Aggie nor Alex replied.

"They're still conducting aerial searches of the area," said the officer with an almost disinterested sigh. "The terrain has not yet been reopened for a ground search, but you will be informed if there is any sign of your brother."

"What the hell happened out there?" said Margot.

The officer flipped his notepad shut. "Erosion and bad timing. From what I've heard, the northernmost end has been badly worn for twenty years. A cave-in at the Cannon Caves set off a series of collapses and boom, boom, boom. Down comes the whole shebang."

He said he was sorry for their loss and opted to show himself out.

"They're still looking," said Margot, trying to sound upbeat, the moment the door was closed. "They'll find him."

That night, Aggie told Alex what happened to Bailey, and Alex—who had never kept a secret from his wife in his life—told Margot the next morning as they sat around the kitchen table, after the kids had gone outside to play. Once they'd finished, Margot had leaned back in her chair, staring at her husband.

"You still have this tape?" She had no reason not to believe them.

"Yes," said Aggie.

"You should destroy it."

A week had passed and in that time it was decided that Aggie would move in with Alex and Margot while she was in recovery. When she was ready, she could either take up the same editing work again or find something new, if she liked. There were more options open to her in a city. Eventually she would find her own place.

"Hope you're not just trying to keep an extra close eye on me," she told Alex the first day they arrived back at her apartment.

He shook his head. "If anything, you'll be watching my back."

They had started on the work of clearing the apartment that day. The TV, the VCR, and the tape still concealed within, watched their progress, the glass of the screen reflecting and distorting their labour.

Aggie was aware that she had not yet cried for Bailey, that she had not even begun to process that unnatural thing that had happened to and perhaps somewhere was still happening to them. Because she had no doubt that the doubles of themselves she had seen and heard were real. That the power in that landscape might hold on to a moment when conditions were just right and replay it over and over like a bad memory in the dark of night seemed certain. It held every choice, leading to a point where only one conclusion could be true. She did not know for certain, but the thought that they were still there, parts of them still walking through those trees, the end forever just out of reach, woke her up in a cold, cloying sweat almost nightly. She had not asked him, but she knew that Alex was having nightmares, too. She hoped one day they would pass.

Alex carried a pair of boxes to the bedroom. Most of her clothes were already in garbage bags, ready for donation.

Everything she planned on keeping could fit into one overnight bag.

Aggie sat quietly at her desk for a full minute, listening to the work coming from the other room, and then got up and went to the TV. She had done this twice before, but never with Alex present. She wondered if it would make a difference.

The dust on the screen crackled as she turned on the old TV. The tape was still in the VCR, and it clunked and whined as she hit power. There was a low, fluttering buzz like a bumblebee caught in the speaker, and then the picture shivered to life.

An overhead view, the moth, and then Joanne stepping out from the trail. Aggie's eyes moved momentarily to the time stamp, confirming that the counter was still going up, that the date was today's.

Joanne moved a strand of hair from her eyes, then looked around at a sound. A figure appeared at the dark end of the path. Joanne paused but as he approached, she relaxed. Bailey stepped into the lamplight and wrapped his arms around her. There they swayed for a moment before he took her hand and they walked out of the shot, down the service road.

Ten seconds later, Joanne was back at the trailhead.

Aggie carefully went around the room and began to pack or throw away items, referring to the tape that had for twenty years been charged by the lodestone of the park. The park was gone, the tape remained. She had read once that the mind could not tell the difference between the memory of an event and the event itself. The tape was a living memory. But like a memory, it could be altered or become faulty, affected by choices.

The first time she had rewatched the tape, she had been paralyzed by grief and terror. The next, she was unpacking everything, deciding in a moment of panic that she could not leave. It was then the tape changed. Joanne had run from the woods—as they'd seen before—but this time Bailey was with her, both of them hurt and both of them trying to outrun the thing chasing them. When she was able to pull herself together, resume packing, take the steps Aggie knew she needed taking, the happy reunion resumed, and they were a step closer to finding the road out. Her choices rippled out. Some were better than others. Sometimes it took longer for Joanne and Bailey to reappear on the trailhead; sometimes they made it further down the road.

Aggie threw away another stack, one less thing to carry. She could not take these things with her, and she could not live her life in here, not when there were roads to travel.

They had found the road; one day they might step off it. And she would be there to greet them with arms free.

ACKNOWLEDGEMENTS

There are several people I'd like to acknowledge who, directly or indirectly, either contributed to this book or to the making of me as a writer.

My husband, John C. Carroll, who has never once doubted me and is the solid ground I need when my head gets too deep in the clouds. This book is for you. I love you. Johnny, for making sure mama was up at the crack of dawn to write this novella. You inspire me every day. My parents, Grace, Dan, and David, for your love and support and teaching me what perseverance looks like. My sisters, Kathleen, Breanna, and Anna for always being there when I need you. Marg, by best friend and truest confidant. Jackie and Dan for many nights with good food, drink, and conversation. Shawn Corey, my high school English teacher, for believing in me before I did. Kevin Whitten (Well-Read Beard) provided the beta-read of this book, and his keen eye helped to spot and smooth the bumps and get this story on more even terrain. All the early readers and reviewers who took the time to see Aggie, Alex, and Bailey to the end, in particular Laurel Hightower, Caitlin Marceau, Sofia Ajram, Ai Jiang, Jarret Middleton, Jacquelyn Benson, and Tim McGregor. Your kindness and enthusiasm make this solitary job a community and I'm grateful for you. Trevor Henderson, thank you for your beautiful and eye-catching art. Alex Woodroe and Matt Blairstone, thank you for giving this story a perfect home, I couldn't have hoped for a more passionate creative team. And finally, my cats Newt and Ripley, my constant companions and lap warmers on cold winter mornings. You cannot read, so I will deliver my appreciation by way of all the good treats.

ABOUT THE CONTRIBUTORS

Laura Keating hails from St. Andrew, New Brunswick and writes about monsters both human and unnatural. Her work has been published by Grindhouse Press, Cemetery Gates, Ghost Orchid Press, and more. Currently, she resides in Montreal with her husband, son, two cats, and possibly one ghost. Follow her on Twitter @lorekeating, or at www.lorekeating.com.

Trevor Henderson is a writer and illustrator. His love of monsters, cryptids, ghosts and other horrible entities is enduring and vast. When he is not drawing or writing horrible things, he is thinking about the unknowable and hostile forces working against all of humanity, and playing with his cat, who is named Boo.
More at www.trevorhenderson.com.

ABOUT TENEBROUS PRESS

Tenebrous Press was conceived in the Plague Year 2020 and unleashed, howling and feral, in spring 2021 to deliver the finest in transgressive, progressive Horror from diverse and unsung voices around the world.

We welcome the esoteric; the unorthodox; the finest in New Weird Horror.

FIND OUT MORE:
www.tenebrouspress.com
Twitter: @TenebrousPress

NEW WEIRD HORROR

CPSIA information can be obtained
at www.ICGtesting.com
Printed in the USA
BVHW072306240323
661100BV00001B/6